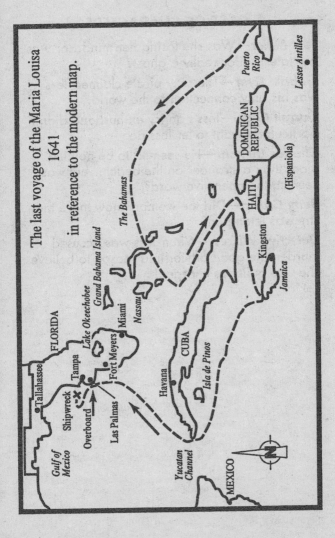

The last voyage of the Maria Louisa
1641
in reference to the modern map.

FLORIDA

Gulf of Mexico

Tallahassee

Tampa

Shipwreck

Overboard

Las Palmas

Fort Meyers

Miami

Lake Okeechobee

Grand Bahama Island

The Bahamas

Nassau

Havana

CUBA

Isla de Pinos

Kingston

Jamaica

HAITI

DOMINICAN REPUBLIC

(Hispaniola)

Puerto Rico

Lesser Antilles

Yucatan Channel

MEXICO

N

CAST OF CHARACTERS

Tess Miller—Was she losing her mind...or was her latest suitor really a ghost?

Gabriel Dyer—The sexy pirate claimed Tess was his only connection to the world.

Darrell Cage—Tess's angry ex-husband didn't particularly want to let Tess go.

Charles Dumont—He seemed to be nothing more than a stranger on the beach...but was *seemed* the operative word?

Betty Crown—Did the woman know more than she was letting on?

Detective Wilkes—When Tess was accused of murder, the good officer had reason to believe she was guilty as charged!

"The only warmth I can feel is your warmth," Gabriel whispered huskily.

Tess could merely stare at this strange man, this apparition dressed in pirate's clothes. Was he a ghost? A time traveler?

"Your skin has the texture of the finest silk," he continued, "and nothing else has any texture at all. You feel complete beneath my hand. And I feel a connection to you. Don't you feel a bit of the same?"

"Yes," Tess whispered, barely able to believe this was actually happening. "But I don't know why."

"A person can grow old waiting to find out the why of things."

"I thought you were a hallucination," she blurted out. "I thought I was losing my mind. Why have you come to me, Gabriel?"

"Ah, Tess," Gabriel returned softly. "Because you're my only connection to the world."

ABOUT THE AUTHOR

Between her writing and children, Laura Pender is kept very busy. She lives in the Minneapolis, Minnesota, area, and she feels that her spouse is a heavy contributor to all her Intrigue novels. A prolific writer, she has written for *Alfred Hitchcock's Mystery Magazine* and many other publications.

Books by Laura Pender

HARLEQUIN INTRIGUE

62—TASTE OF TREASON
70—HIT AND RUN
91—TRAITOR'S DISPATCH
108—SKY PIRATE
142—DEJA VU
177—MINDGAME
212—DANGEROUS VINTAGE
240—GARDEN OF DECEIT
249—MUSIC OF THE MIST
280—MIDNIGHT RIDER
292—THE DREAMER'S KISS

Don't miss any of our special offers. Write to us at the following address for information on our newest releases.

Harlequin Reader Service
U.S.: 3010 Walden Ave., P.O. Box 1325, Buffalo, NY 14269
Canadian: P.O. Box 609, Fort Erie, Ont. L2A 5X3

The Pirate Ghost

Laura Pender

Harlequin Books

TORONTO • NEW YORK • LONDON
AMSTERDAM • PARIS • SYDNEY • HAMBURG
STOCKHOLM • ATHENS • TOKYO • MILAN
MADRID • WARSAW • BUDAPEST • AUCKLAND

ISBN 0-373-22368-4

THE PIRATE GHOST

This edition published by arrangement with Harlequin Books S.A.

® and TM are trademarks of the publisher. Trademarks indicated with
® are registered in the United States Patent and Trademark Office, the
Canadian Trade Marks Office and in other countries.

Printed in U.S.A.

Chapter One

It was after midnight when Tess Miller parked her car in the lot at Bernie's Lounge, a beachfront tavern in Los Palmas, Florida, and got out. It was a beautiful, moonless night, the clear sky alive with stars. Tess stood for a moment looking up at those distant points of light visible beyond the lights of the nightclub before walking down to the sand. She wasn't going to the bar, but merely borrowing a space in their lot while she strolled along the broad beach that graced the shore of the Gulf of Mexico.

She'd given up a beachfront home in her recent divorce and found herself landlocked now, after five years with an ocean view. The beach was the only thing she missed about her marriage to Darrell Cage, and so she had made it a practice to return to it for a stroll before bed a couple nights a week. Even though it meant a drive across town for the pleasure, she loved the serenity of the ocean lying dark beneath the stars. And, on a moonless night like tonight, the mystery of the ocean filled her with a sense of awe that soothed her after a hard day's work.

The tall, athletic brunette took off her white canvas shoes and walked north from the nightclub, surveying the ocean with calm brown eyes. There was something about the endless expanse of water that drew her back, a nameless feeling of desire that seemed imposed from the outside and totally separate from her own feelings. It was as if the ocean itself was calling to her, and she always answered the call.

But the disturbing thought of Darrell Cage, her ex-husband, came unbidden. His large house was just south of here. It was most emphatically his house—never really hers. Just as she had been his wife—his property as far as he was concerned. It had taken her five years to realize that about him. Five years to realize that his big house and his money couldn't make her happy.

She had hoped that a child would bring them closer but her pregnancy had ended in a miscarriage. Darrell had told her they hadn't really wanted kids yet anyway, and then he had gone out on "business" and left her alone again. How could she have ever loved him? How could he have been so unfeeling?

Memories were stubborn things. But it was all in the past now. After the long fight to divorce herself from that possessive, vindictive man, Tess had her life back, and Darrell Cage was just one more bad memory.

There were nothing but good memories ahead of her now.

Tess walked along the beach, beyond the lights of the beach strip, then toward the private beach. It fronted the expensive homes on Sandhook Road, where the movers and shakers of Los Palmas lived. There were lights on in some of the big houses, but none that extended far enough to illuminate the shoreline.

Tess reached a small cluster of water-smoothed rocks and sat down to rest. She'd walked much farther than she had intended, and she felt flushed and hot. A smile skated over her lips. What she needed was a cooling dip in the placid gulf waters.

For a moment, it seemed as though a lilting masculine voice was calling her name, beckoning her to come into the ocean's cool depths. And why not? The beach was deserted and she was a strong swimmer; why not follow her whim?

Tess glanced around quickly, then dropped her shoes beside the rock and stripped to her underclothes. From a distance, she'd look as if she were wearing a swimsuit. She ran eagerly to the beckoning waters and dived in.

The water refreshed her with its cool touch, and she rolled over onto her back and floated, looking up at the stars. Then, feeling energetic and carefree, she turned over and took several strong strokes just to enjoy exerting her muscles. She dived beneath the surface and then burst up again, winded and happy. She had lettered in swimming in high school, placing third in the freestyle event in the state competition during her senior year, but that had been ten years ago and it felt good to know she still remembered her training.

Rolling onto her back again, Tess floated easily, sculling her hands just enough to keep herself afloat until she decided to head back to shore. She turned over and treaded water, looking for land.

She couldn't find the shore at first, and a flutter of panic struck her when she found herself in a dark world without a reference point to guide her. Then, what sounded like a shout caught her ear. She turned toward the noise. Yes, a rectangle of light had appeared in one of the houses on what must be the shore. She could dimly see two figures standing in it. Were they really that far away? Suddenly, the light was extinguished, but she had her bearings now. She began swimming toward shore.

You forgot about the tide, she thought as she swam. It had still been going out when she'd started swimming. Now, she was much farther out than she'd intended to go, way too far.

She swam faster, fighting against the fear that coiled in the pit of her stomach. Taking strong strokes, she kicked hard. When she paused to catch her breath, she looked around her. She could see the darker shape of land against the dark sky now, so she knew she'd made progress, but she was still dreadfully far out.

She swam again, slower now, knowing that endurance was the key rather than speed. It seemed to take forever, and she was dizzy with fatigue, but the next time she looked, the land was closer, looming large before her. She could make it now. She would be all right.

Finally, she felt something with the tip of her toe. When she swam a bit farther, her toe dragged through sand and over a rough bit of rock. She was almost there!

Too tired to swim anymore, Tess put her feet down. She was barely able to keep her head out of the water when she stood on tiptoe. Suddenly, a swell of water rushed over her, filling her mouth and nose and knocking her off balance.

Tess panicked, thrashing in the water. Then she broke free, coughing and sputtering, only to be pulled down by another swell. The sandy bottom beneath her feet vanished. And there didn't seem to be any up or down in the dark water, no light and no air, no safety.

She broke the surface one more time, drawing in a breath that choked her and burned her chest, shouting once, feebly, "Help me!"

But no one was there and she sank again.

And then there was little sensation, nothing but the grip of the dark gulf waters and the painful beat of her heart. Nothing but the ocean, deep and cold. Miles of water and icy silence. Only quiet death lay beneath these waves.

But she seemed to hear the sound of a ship's bell— an old-fashioned dinging like that of a sailing ship. She could swear she heard men shouting. They sounded terrified, and the roar of an ocean storm was swirling around them. But then all sounds faded— except the sound of her heart and a man calling her name from the depths.

She felt herself miraculously rising in the water. She felt the cool touch of air on her face and shoulders, the warm strength of a man's arms around her back and the strong movement of his thighs against her as he carried her up from the water.

She coughed—water erupted from her mouth and was replaced by feeble currents of air. And then she was laid on the sand.

"Have you no sense?" A man's deep, lilting voice broke through the ragged sound of her own breathing. "Swimming in the moonlight like an eel. No, floundering like a pup in a sack, you were, for it wasn't swimming. You'da drowned surely if you hadn't woke me, and a beauty like yourself deserves better than to end up blue on the rocks somewhere."

She couldn't speak. It was all she could do to breathe just then. Each gasp of air burned her chest and rasped in her throat. So, she could only lie on the sand and stare, blinking, at the dark form of the man above her.

"Don't try talking, lass," he said softly. "And, anyway, it's me who should be thanking you."

As Tess's senses slowly returned, she could make out a square-cut face with a rather broad nose poised above the friendliest smile she'd ever seen. Green eyes, she thought. They sparkled like emeralds in his shadowed face.

"Thank you anyway," she said now. She swallowed hard; it hurt to talk.

"And thank you," he replied. Then he leaned down and slipped one hand behind her head, lifting it toward his. "Such a beautiful woman, you are. A comely lass such as yourself should sleep with someone other than Davey Jones.''

He kissed her then, claiming her lips roughly as his due for his heroism. Then he drew back and released her with a laugh. His wet skin gleamed as he sat back on his haunches, highlighting a bare, muscular chest and stomach.

''That's all the thanks I'll ask for now,'' he said. ''Though, seeing you like this, I'll admit I'm cursing myself for being a gentleman. But a gentleman I'll stay, and I'll bid a good-night to you.''

Suddenly, she realized he was naked! Seemingly unconcerned, he turned with a small shake of his head and walked back toward the ocean.

Tess lifted herself up on her elbows, trying to call out to the man. But her voice was gone, scoured away by salt water. She was helpless to do anything but watch the man walk away, the long mane of his ponytail hanging halfway down his back. He walked directly into the sea without looking back, continuing until the water rose up and consumed him.

She fell weakly back onto the sand. Within moments, she fell blessedly asleep. Her savior was waiting in the gray shadows of her dreams, where he seemed more substantial than he had on the shore. His body was hard with well-worked muscles, his eyes a soft green and his smile as gentle as a baby's.

''Should you need me, lass, just call for Gabriel Dyer,'' he said, nestling his mouth close to her ear. ''Now that you've found me, I'll come running. Lord knows I couldn't help myself in any case from running after so fair a lady. Dead or not, I surely couldn't help it at all.''

His words remained after he'd gone, lulling her with their secure promise, borne on the sound of waves and the creaking of ancient rigging as sails moved in the gentle gulf breeze that flowed through her dream.

Chapter Two

Tess awoke shivering as the frail rays of dawn filtered past the big houses on the shore and over the placid water. She was disoriented, unsure of where she was, but when she rolled to her side and felt the damp sand beneath her hands, she remembered.

"Oh, no," she moaned. Her head throbbed as though a heavy-metal band was warming up inside it, and her legs felt like ice. Her long dark hair was matted with sand, her mouth tasted of seawater and her throat hurt horribly. "What did you do to yourself?" she sighed as she pushed herself up to her knees.

And then she remembered. Thank heavens someone had been swimming just where she needed him to be. It didn't seem possible that anyone else could have been in the water but he must have been, since she surely hadn't saved herself. She felt like a total fool for having been caught by the tide. She could have been drowned through her foolishness.

And now, she was in a real pickle. She was half-clothed on a strange beach and the sun was coming up. She had to find her clothing fast!

Unfortunately, the tide had come in while she slept, and her purse and clothing weren't in sight. Tess stood quickly and scanned the beach. She spotted something! Yes, a shoe, and she ran to it despite the hammering behind her anxious brown eyes. Her other shoe lay just beyond it, and beyond that she saw her blouse. She shook it out quickly, struggled into the damp garment and buttoned it.

Fortunately, her shirttails were long. She looked as if she might be wearing a beach cover-up. Taking her shoes in one hand, she walked farther along toward a pile of smooth boulders. She didn't have much hope of finding her blue jeans, but she found her purse lying half-buried in the sand. Inside, she found her car keys.

At least she'd be able to drive home. It was early yet and all she had to do was get to her car without being seen. She might make it. Hoping to preserve some dignity, Tess began walking along the shore as though she was just out for a stroll.

"This is a private beach, you know." A man's voice stopped her. "Not that I mind."

Was it her savior from last night? She turned to look at the man. He approached her rapidly; he seemed to come from a two-story house of glass and weathered wood that was perched on a low hill. He was tall, with sandy hair and a saltwater tan, and he was wearing a pair of brown Dockers and a blue crewneck shirt. He caught up to her, his smile revealing a set of glistening white teeth. He had blue eyes, though. So it hadn't been him last night.

"Technically, the beach is public," she replied hoarsely. "But I'm leaving it nonetheless." Tess cleared her throat and shook her hair back as best she could while she continued walking toward the beach area in front of Bernie's Lounge. It seemed a horribly long way off.

"Like I said, I don't mind," he told her, walking at her side. "You look as though you slept out here."

"And you look as though you didn't," she said. "What of it?"

"Do you make a practice of sleeping on the beach? Or did your date desert you?"

"I didn't have a date," she retorted. "And I think I'm far enough away from your house now, so you can chill."

"How can I relax with a beautiful woman so near?"

As she walked, a dark spot on the shore began to come into her view. Drawing closer, she saw that it was her jeans, a sight she would have welcomed moments earlier. Now, however, her dignity might be better served by leaving them. It was no time to admit that the empress had no clothes, so she walked past them, regretting only the loss of the spare change in her pocket.

"Well, if you decide you might *want* a date," he persisted, "give me a call. Charles Dumont."

"I'll remember that, Charlie," Tess said, smiling his way. "But I've got an appointment, so please excuse me."

"Certainly," he said. "I'm just out for a stroll myself."

"Right." They had reached Bernie's, and Tess started up the slope to the parking lot. "Goodbye."

"Goodbye." Charles Dumont remained on the beach and watched her walk up to the lot. "See you soon," he called out.

Tess didn't reply but hurried up the slope. Once she was in the parking lot, she ran across the asphalt to her car and threw herself inside. *Never again, never again,* she thought as she started the engine and threw the dusty blue Toyota into gear. *I'll do my swimming in the public pool.* She could feel herself blushing hotly now, feeling as though everyone she passed along the route home was staring at her and clucking their tongues in remonstration. *Never, never, never again.*

ONCE SHE WAS SAFELY HOME and standing under the hot spray of her shower, she began to find a bit of humor in her situation. It could have been worse after all. She might have drowned and her body washed out to sea.

And if that had happened, and they found no sign of her but her purse lying on the beach, they'd assume she had committed suicide. She'd be remembered as a woman who just couldn't face life without Darrell Cage. Now that was a far worse fate than to be caught on the beach in her underwear. She'd rather be caught naked with her face painted blue than to have anyone think that.

Thinking of it that way, her night's adventure hadn't been all that bad. She'd survived her ordeal with no worse damage than some sand in her hair after all. That could be washed away.

She wished she could wash Darrell Cage out of her hair as easily, but even he would eventually tire of trying to get her back. Even he must realize that she didn't need him for anything.

Of course, in the daylight, she was able to remember some nice things about the man. When he hadn't been drinking, he was almost charming. He could flatter a woman out of anything and make her feel like the center of his universe. Darrell was a charmer and a good provider. His real-estate business covered most of the Gulf Coast, earning him a substantial income.

It was just too bad that he had seen her simply as a possession. It was also too bad he didn't know the first thing about love.

But now she was free. She'd even done without alimony—so far. He'd offered a great deal, but she wanted him completely out of her life.

The memory of Darrell chilled her. It made her think of the baby, too. Had she gone full term, her child would have been over a year old by now, and she didn't want to think about that. No, her life was in the present.

She turned off the shower and stepped out to towel herself dry. She left the bathroom toweling her hair and walked across the hall to her bedroom. Glancing at her naked body in the mirror above her dresser, she thought about the man on the beach again. He had, apparently, been skinny-dipping last night and wasn't the least bit embarrassed about it. Nor was he flaunting his nakedness; he simply was as he was. How she wished she were that much at ease with anything in her life.

But who was he? He intrigued her, this vision of strength and certitude rising to her aid like a sea god and then returning to his domain when his task was completed. She wished she could remember more of what he said, but the memory of his kiss had left her grasping for the threads of his words.

The man had not just kissed her, but he'd taken her lips as though they were due him. It wasn't the kind of taking that Darrell had done, either. This man had shown restraint. The liberty of a kiss and nothing more. She had been in no condition to stop him if he'd had more predatory intentions. But he was a gentleman. At least as much as a man could be in such a situation.

And what had he said? What was his name? She was sure she had been told, but the memory slipped from her mind like everything else he'd said. The more she tried to remember, the harder it was to do so.

Tess dressed herself in a pair of blue running shorts and a tank top and then went into the kitchen where she made herself a light breakfast of toast and coffee. She took her plate and cup to the breakfast nook overlooking her small, fenced-in yard and sat to read the Sunday paper.

Although the house she rented was small, it was a friendly space and it was hers. That was all she had asked for. The furnishings, which she'd rented along with the house, weren't all to her taste, but they were serviceable pieces.

Thank God I'm not in here, she thought as she read the paper. She could imagine the report. "Woman missing, feared dead. Purse found on beach."

All at once, the man's words rushed back to her. "Now that you've found me, I'll come running." That was what he had said. "Just call for..."

Call for whom? She still couldn't remember his name. All she could really remember was his face and the Irish lilt of his voice.

"Just call for..."

God, how she wished she could remember his name.

Her doorbell rang, startling her. She didn't normally have visitors on a Sunday morning. Normally she'd be in church. But this wasn't a normal Sunday. After one quick sip of coffee, Tess hurried to the door.

"Coming," she called. When she threw open the door, she felt truly disinclined toward company.

"Hello." Charles Dumont, the man who had surprised her on the beach that morning, was standing on her small porch with a paper bag in one hand and a large smile lighting his amiable features. "So, we meet again."

"It appears so. What on earth are you doing here?" she asked, taken aback by his appearance at her home. "And how did you find me?"

"Well, let's see." He opened the bag and withdrew the contents—her denim jeans freshly laundered. He chuckled. "I thought it would be nice if I brought your jeans back to you."

"Those aren't mine," she said quickly, regretting the foolish lie immediately.

"No? Gee, then I guess whoever lost these jeans must have stolen your credit card." He took a card from the breast pocket of his shirt and read the name aloud. "Teresa Cage?"

Tess stared at the card for a moment, remembering with sudden clarity that she'd bought gas with the plastic and slipped the card into the back pocket of her jeans rather than fumble with her purse.

"Teresa Miller," she said then, somewhat sheepishly. "But, yes, that's my card."

"And these?"

"All right. They're my jeans. Thank you very much for returning them to me." She accepted the garment and credit card from the man as graciously as she could.

"It was no problem at all," he said. "I smell coffee."

"The gulf air must sharpen your senses," she replied stonily. But then she smiled, relenting. "So, could I offer you a cup?"

"I don't mind if I do." He smiled again and folded the grocery bag neatly as he accepted the invitation and followed her into the house. "Nice place. Comfortable," he observed.

"Rented," she returned. "With rented furniture."

"That explains the fly-fishing pictures on the wall."

"I haven't been here very long. How do you take your coffee?"

"Black, no sugar, thank you."

They walked through her kitchen, then took their cups to the breakfast nook and sat across from each other at the small table.

"So, what do you do for a living, Mr. Dumont?" Tess asked.

"Please, it was Charlie this morning," he said.

"I wasn't feeling very chipper earlier."

"And now that you're feeling better, you're inclined to be more formal?"

"I—no, but I don't know you."

"Okay, fair enough. My name is Charlie Dumont, and I'm a banker. While I might make some joke about 'Mr.' Dumont being my father, I don't recall anyone calling my father 'Mr.,' either. He was a banker, too, and everyone called him Ted. We're an old New England family who made our money in the Boston area. I've recently moved south because I wanted to enjoy a bit of our accumulated wealth rather than spend all of my time accumulating more." He paused, sipping his coffee. "Let's see, I think that's the basic outline. Will you drop the Mr. Dumont business now?"

"I think that's enough to move on to Charles, yes," she said, laughing. "Why on earth did you drive across town to bring me these things?"

"It was a beautiful Sunday morning for a drive," he answered. "I didn't mind."

"Thank you again." She didn't know what else to say. Though he was good-looking and well spoken, she was hardly interested in starting any new relationships.

"So how did you manage to land on our beach this morning?"

He, apparently, wasn't at a loss for words and was determined to have a conversation.

"That's none of your business," she said.

"I know I'm being nosy," he admitted over his coffee. "But when I see a beautiful woman on my beach, I get curious."

"Oh, you do? I would think it happens all the time," Tess replied, smiling innocently. "Besides, why were you up and around so early in the morning? Dawn is hardly banker's hours. Maybe I'm curious, too."

"I always get up early," he said easily. "A family trait, really. My father is a bird-watcher, always up at the crack of dawn with his binoculars. I guess it's genetic."

"Bird-watching?"

"Very funny," he said, amused. "But Dumonts do tend to rise early for whatever reason. You're quick. I like that."

"You've made my day. But to tell the truth, I'm not really feeling much up to company today."

"Hangovers can be painful, can't they?"

"I'm not hung over."

"My mistake." He laughed and finished his coffee. "Well, hey, I'll leave you alone for now, but I'd appreciate your company for dinner this evening if you can make it."

"Well, I do have to eat," she said. "But I was rather looking forward to a TV dinner tonight."

"Postpone it," he returned. "We'll have a quiet meal and I'll get you home early. Tomorrow is a working day after all."

"Okay, I'll leave my supper in the freezer and trust you to know a good restaurant."

"I can think of a couple." He stood then, smiling warmly. "Shall I come for you at seven?"

"Sure, if that's when you get here."

"It's a date, then. Well, goodbye, Teresa Miller."

"Goodbye, Charlie Dumont."

Tess walked the man out of her house thinking that life did, indeed, move in strange ways. Last night, she nearly drowned, and now she had a dinner invitation from a good-looking and very eligible young banker.

And then there was the matter of her mysterious rescuer. He was the person who intrigued her even more. Despite Charles Dumont's charm and good looks, she couldn't help but compare him with the half-remembered image of the man on the beach. Where Charles seemed to be a nice man, the other was...

Well, he had something special. She couldn't describe it, but she could see and hear it in her mind. It was the glint of green in his eyes and the Irish lilt of his voice; it was the sure strength of his limbs and the kindly restraint of his gentlemanly manner. It was all of that as well as the feeling that he was someone she had been waiting for without ever knowing it.

As she closed the door behind her visitor, she realized that she'd trade a dinner with Charlie Dumont just to remember the name of the man who'd saved her.

All she needed to know was his name.

Chapter Three

The Gulf Shore Club was a bit fancier a place than Tess had expected when Charles Dumont asked her out for dinner, but she had fortunately overruled her first inclination and dressed in a black dress rather than slacks and a blouse. They were seated at a table with a perfect view of the gulf, and it seemed that Charles was well-known and important.

"I neglected to ask what you do for a living, Teresa," he said, his smile brightening, when he mentioned her name.

"I'm an accountant," she told him. "I keep books for a small manufacturing company here in Los Palmas."

"An accountant. Then we're in the same field."

"Except that the only banking I do is when they tell me my checking account is overdrawn."

Charles laughed, nestling comfortably back in his chair as he watched her. "You don't do the payroll at your company?"

"No, we have an office manager who handles that. I take care of sales accounts."

"If you're ever looking to move up, please do think of me. I never seem to have enough accountants."

"Do you mean a personal accountant?" she asked with an impertinent tilt of her head.

"Any position you might like, of course." He turned toward the approaching wine steward with a welcoming smile. "A white wine, I think," he said to Tess as the man came up to the table. "Do you agree?"

"Yes, white wine," Tess said. "But just a glass."

Charles shot her a look of playful censure and ordered a bottle. "So," he said, "are you hungry?"

"Ravenous," she replied.

"They have a fine selection of seafood." He opened his menu. "I can't really recommend the beef. Nothing out of the ordinary there anyway."

"I'll let you decide," she said with a smile.

"We'll just have a look, then," he said, grinning over the menu. "Crab sounds nice, no, lobster. Yes, because I always embarrass myself fighting with crab. Is lobster all right?"

"Fine."

The setting sun was creating a beautiful scene of reflected glory on the ocean beyond the window. Its low-angled rays cast shadows that reached for the golden light that struck the waves. A pair of children were at play on the sandy shore—two dark shapes chasing a ball around. In another moment, the sun would be gone.

"So," he said, "were you on the beach all night? It was certainly a lovely night for it."

"Charlie, I'd rather not go into it."

"I don't mean to pry, but if you were stranded, I could have at least offered you a couch to sleep on."

"If you must know, I went for a swim and the tide took me a bit too far from shore. I nearly drowned trying to get back. And when I did, I passed out on the beach," Tess said impatiently. "There, that's all there is to it."

"The tide took you out?" Charles's eyes widened with concern, though his tone remained even. "This night-swimming habit of yours could be fatal. Do you know people on the beach? Friends?"

"No, I don't know a soul there," she said, "and it's not a habit. It was just a whim."

"It must have been hard to get your bearings on a moonless night like that."

"That was the problem. Everyone had their lights off, and I was too low in the water to make out shapes on the horizon. I was lucky someone turned his deck light on for a moment so I could see my way."

Charles frowned, tracing his finger over the rim of his wineglass. "And here I've been teasing you about it when it was really quite an ordeal."

"It's all past now."

"Whose light was it? Do you know?"

"No, but I swam straight toward it." Tess tasted her wine. "It might even have been your light. Were you awake that late?"

"No." Charles shook his head quickly. "I'm up with the birds, remember?"

"Oh, yes. You like to get out right away to see what the tide washes in."

"And I had quite a find today, didn't I?"

Tess chuckled, even though she was beginning to suspect he was the blunt, nosy type, who couldn't help prying. "I did meet a neighbor of yours last night," she said, trying to both keep the conversation moving and hide her curiosity.

"Oh, really?" Charles said. "Who?"

"I didn't get his name, or rather, I don't remember what he told me. Anyway, an Irishman." She smiled, the man's voice coming back to her as she spoke. "Do you know him?"

"Can't think of any Irishmen near me." Charles was frowning, apparently taking inventory of his neighbors. "No, none that I can think of. How did you meet him?"

"On the beach, earlier," she lied. She didn't want to carry the conversation back to her foolish swim. "You know, I think I do remember his name. It was something with a *D*, Donnell or O'Donnell. No, it was Dyer!" she exclaimed triumphantly. "Is there a Dyer near you?"

"No," he stated positively. "There isn't any Dyer."

His frown had deepened as though the mention of another man had dampened his enthusiasm for the conversation. Nevertheless, Tess felt strangely happy about remembering her benefactor's last name.

"I assumed that he lived nearby," she went on. "But then that isn't necessarily the case, is it? I don't live there after all."

"It is a nice location," Charles said. "And, as you pointed out, the beach is public."

"No, I don't imagine he lives in the neighborhood at all," she said then, noticing her dinner partner's distraction. "You said you came here for the sun, but did you bring any business with you?"

"Sure. It's a global market now. Anyplace with a fax machine and a modem is as good as the home office. Location isn't as important as influence and information."

"So you moved here just for personal reasons."

"Right. I like the climate here much more than in Boston."

"I don't blame you. I'm from Connecticut originally, but I've gotten used to the climate here."

"Why did you move down?"

"I married a Floridian. He worked in Tampa."

"But you're no longer married?"

"No, I'm no longer married," she said simply. "But I'm going to stay put."

"Maybe I will, too," he said, gazing deeply into her eyes. "I think I like the people here."

Tess smiled, feeling uncomfortable under his scrutiny even though his was a friendly gaze. She found his attentions somewhat suspicious, though she didn't really know why. Maybe it wasn't him she didn't trust, but herself. Now that the divorce was final, she'd intended to remain free of men for a while. But here she was dining with a wealthy young banker while entertaining less than platonic thoughts about some stranger on the beach last night.

Fortunately, their meal arrived. It wasn't until after dinner that Charles began to get personal again. He raised his glass toward her and said, "I've enjoyed the evening."

"I have, too," Tess replied honestly. "I haven't been out in a while."

"I'd like to see to it that you get out more." His voice was soft, a masculine purr that resonated deep within her. "What are you doing tomorrow night?"

"Well, I don't know," she said uncertainly.

Before she could offer an excuse to slow down the progression of intimacy, he asked, "How about dinner at my place?"

"Oh, I don't think so. I enjoyed tonight, but I'm not up to socializing every night."

"And I thought I was being quite charming and gentlemanly." He smiled as he spoke, but the tightness of the smile betrayed a certain inner tension.

"You were a perfect gentleman," Tess returned.

"Then come to dinner. I know how to continue being a gentleman. Or, we could go out again."

"It's not that," Tess said quickly. "It's just that, well, I was married for five years. Five years of seeing the same man every day."

"I wasn't asking for a permanent commitment," he countered. "Just a dinner date."

"I know, but going out again so soon feels awkward to me."

"Okay, Tuesday. What about Tuesday?"

"Oh, all right." Tess laughed at his speedy accommodation to her terms. "Tuesday would be nice."

"Wonderful. Now, since tomorrow is a workday, I suppose it would only be fair to get you home early."

"I am a bit tired."

"Well, then, we'll get the check and be on our way."

CHARLES PARKED HIS CAR in front of her bungalow and clasped her hand in his before she could open the car door. "I had a wonderful evening," he said again quietly. "And I hope that you did, as well."

"I certainly did, Charles. I'm glad you caught me on your beach."

"Me, too."

He dipped his head toward hers and kissed her quickly, his move catching her off guard. "What time should I come for you on Tuesday?" he asked, a note of determination coloring his voice now.

"Seven would be fine," Tess said. "I work close by, so it won't take long to get ready."

"Great." He opened his car door and hurried around to meet her as she opened her door and stepped out. "You might want to bring a bathing suit, too." When they reached her front door, he said, "Good night, Tess. I'll see you on Tuesday."

"Good night."

She watched him walk back to his car, feeling strangely uncertain about the man. There wasn't anything wrong with him and he hadn't behaved badly, yet she wasn't terribly eager to see him again. What was it about him that put her on guard like this?

Unlocking the door to her dark house, Tess decided that it probably wasn't him as much as all men she was on guard against. Maybe the problem was the shadowy man named Dyer.

She knew even less about Dyer than she did about Charles Dumont but she felt that she could trust him more. While he, too, had stolen a kiss, his had been more graciously bestowed.

Tess changed out of her dinner dress quickly and put on her favorite pair of men's cotton pajamas and a light robe. She'd simply relax for the rest of the evening. She had just begun a new novel and was eager to return to it. Now, if she could only find some relaxing music on the radio, she would brew a cup of tea and settle down for a good read....

But her doorbell rang. She went to answer it with a sigh of resignation. It was probably Betty Crown, a friend from work who was chronically unable to manage her life and who was constantly in a state of alarm. She was about due to come running to Tess for aid and comfort.

But it wasn't Betty. It was Darrell Cage.

"Good evening, dear, glad to catch you in," he said sarcastically as he began to step through the door.

"Hey," Tess shouted, barring his way, "I'm not inviting you in, Darrell."

"Oh, come on, Teresa. What's wrong with my coming in to talk over old times?"

"I've signed all the papers, Darrell. Your precious business is free of any claims from me. The least you can do is let me be free, too. Our divorce is final."

"I'm not here about business, Tess."

"I'm not dressed," she protested, still blocking the door.

"I've seen you in less," he replied with a leer.

"But you won't again," she assured him. "Now go away."

"No." Darrell ducked beneath her arm and stepped into the house. "See? Nothing happened. I'm inside and you're still safe and sound."

"What do you want?" she asked, her tone resigned. "It's nearly ten o'clock."

"But you've never been one for an early bedtime, so I knew it wasn't too late." He sat in a bentwood rocker. "I just wanted to know how your date went."

"What date?"

"The blond twerp who dropped you off half an hour ago—*that* date, dear. How was it?"

"That's none of your business."

"But I remember a whole evening spent with your telling me how I had turned you off men for good. I clearly remember that." He stood quickly and strode over to stand in front of her. "Don't you remember?"

"Yes," she replied, swallowing hard. "So what?"

"So what? So here you are running around town. Even though you spoke out in public and declared that I caused you to be unable to trust men."

"My dating is none of your business," she said again, stepping back from him. "I'm not your wife anymore."

"Three months ago you still were my wife!" he shouted.

"We'd been separated for over a year!"

"Three lousy months! You coulda let the ink dry, Teresa!"

"I did!" she shouted back, loosing her temper. "What's wrong, Darrell? Can't bully me as often as you like? Run out of papers for me to sign so you're left with spying on me to make me miserable?"

"You were my wife!" he repeated angrily, his fists tightening.

"Well, I'm not now!"

"You'll never marry anyone else, Teresa!" he threatened, his voice rising. "I promise you that!"

Seeing the explosive anger in his face, Tess froze. Now she wished she had invited Charles inside and avoided Darrell's jealous outburst. But that would only have postponed the confrontation, and she didn't expect that Charles would have been much of a protector anyway. No, Mr. Dyer might fill that capacity, but Charles Dumont was surely more of a negotiator than a fighter and would be useless against the likes of Darrell.

Darrell stepped up to within a foot of her, backing her against the couch. "Was that the point of the divorce? To get a chance to go out with new men?"

"No, to get away from you," she replied evenly. She wasn't about to back down from him, not now or ever.

"And where is he now? Or maybe he wasn't your type. What kind of man were you looking for when you made up those lies about me and threw them around in public?" He grasped her shoulders.

"Let go of me, you animal!" Tess struggled, trying to escape his hold. "Get out!"

"What kind of man do you want?" His grip on her tightened. "Tell me!"

"Any kind but your kind!" she shouted.

Darrell pushed her away, sending her sprawling to the floor in the center of the room. Shakily, she rose to her knees, weeping.

"A man like Gabriel Dyer," she whispered, marveling at how the name had come to her. "Gabriel Dyer."

"So that's his name!" His eyes glazed, Darrell headed toward her, seeming capable of murder. Suddenly, Tess heard a voice imploring her from behind.

"Use your head, lass," the voice said. "Butt him hard in the stomach! Do it now!"

Without thought, she launched herself forcefully at Darrell's middle and knocked him back against the couch.

"Now cup his ears hard while he's reeling," the man said. "Then twist an arm up behind his back if you can."

Once more, Tess complied, slamming her cupped hands hard against Darrell's ears as he was beginning to rise. Darrell cried out and reached for his ears, but Tess took one wrist in both hands and twisted the arm down and around, pinning him to the floor.

"That's a fine show, lass," Gabriel said. "Fine indeed. But you've got to do better. Pull his arm hard up behind his head or he won't believe you mean business. Hard!" he insisted when she failed to increase the pressure. "Snap it up as if you mean to break it, dear, for you've got to walk him out the door now."

She did as he said, pulling Darrell's arm up until he groaned. Then she pulled until Darrell rose to his feet. She pushed him, half-crouched, toward the front door. A moment later, Darrell was standing in the yard massaging his shoulder.

"You lousy..." he began.

Tess slammed the door, cutting off the rest of his invective. She locked and chained the door and leaned back against it with a thankful sigh. Then she tensed again, suddenly aware of what had just happened.

"Gabriel?" she asked timidly. There was no one to be seen in the room with her. "Gabriel Dyer? Where are you?"

"Right here." The man rose until he was standing in a stooped position behind the large reclining chair she used for reading.

"My goodness, how did you get in? How did you know to come?" Tess began walking toward the man, smiling gratefully even as she began to ask the first of dozens of questions that had suddenly come into her mind.

"Wait there," he commanded, thrusting one palm toward her over the chair. "I haven't a stitch of clothing on me, lass! If you have any modesty, you'd turn out the light!"

"What?" But his chest was indeed bare, so she had no reason to doubt him. "How did you get here naked?"

"It's a long story," he replied, grinning. "So humor me and give me some darkness in lieu of clothing."

In spite of the strange circumstances, she was about to do just that when a singular occurrence stopped her movement back toward the door. When Dyer lowered his hand, it dropped directly through the chair as though it was nothing but a shadow!

Chapter Four

Tess couldn't believe what she'd just seen. His hand hadn't just passed through the chair, had it? No, no way. But then she was neither drunk nor crazy, and she saw what she saw, didn't she? She wasn't really sure at all.

"You are...?" she began. She really wasn't sure what she intended to ask.

"I am what I am, I imagine," he said, smiling. "Naked, mostly, at this time. Could you? The light?"

"Oh, yes." In shock, she switched off the light, the only remaining illumination coming from the hallway light in a long rectangle on the floor.

"There," he said. "I feel better for the darkness. We haven't exactly been properly introduced. My name is Gabriel Dyer."

He extended his hand toward her, and Tess eyed it skeptically. How could she shake hands with a man who couldn't even touch a chair?

"Yes, I know," Tess said. She walked over to him and took his hand, jumping slightly when she found herself holding a very solid and surprisingly warm and strong hand. "I'm Tess Miller."

"And I know that, as well," Gabriel said.

He held her hand a moment longer, looking into her eyes, then released it and crossed his arms over his chest.

"Do that again," Tess said. "What you did earlier. Drop your hands down."

"Oh, that." He did as she asked, and both his hands swung through the chair. He placed them on his hips hidden behind the chair. "I've a bit of a problem getting hold of things, lass," he told her. "Did you think I didn't want to grab the wharf rat that was doing you harm?"

"I hadn't really thought about that," she said, wondering if she was losing her mind. "I'm still trying to understand how you can put your hand through my chair."

"Well, I'm not all here, you might say." He laughed then, filling the air with a musical sound. "What year is it?"

"It's 1995."

"Well, then, my ciphering isn't the best, and long out of practice I am, but I'd say it's been three hundred and fifty odd years since I've managed to touch anything at all. Until you, that is. Aye, I've found I'm well able to touch you, lass."

"Three hundred and fifty?" Whatever this guy was trying to pull on her, it wasn't making sense so far. "What are you talking about?"

"Well, it was September, in the year of our Lord 1641, when my crew threw me from the foredeck of the *Maria Louisa*." He laughed. "That was the end of me for certain."

"What are you talking about?"

"Mutiny," he said, emphasizing the word as though talking to a slow child. "They killed me!"

"Who killed you? No, wait a second. Why should I ask who did it when I can't believe for a moment that it's been done? Killed? You mean killed dead?"

"There's no other type of killed I can think of," he replied easily. "Not in this world anyway."

"But you're here," she said. "I can see you, Gabriel. And I can touch you."

"I'm not conversant with the mechanics of this thing," he said. "I'll admit as much. But the fact remains that they threw me from the ship and left me to drown—which I did, I assure you. Until last night, when you came splashing so close to my own fate, I hadn't made contact with another human being in three hundred and fifty—no, fifty-four years. It's a fact, miss. I'm not lying."

"Get real."

"What is it you're saying?" He cocked his ear toward her in curiosity. Then he smiled, saying, "Oh, that's a current phrase of sorts, I take it. You don't believe me? Well, here, keep your eyes on me, then."

With that, he disappeared.

"Where are you?"

Tess turned around, hoping to catch a glimpse of him running to a hiding place in the room. She saw nothing, but she seemed to feel a breeze and catch the scent of sea air for a moment.

"Okay, I'm impressed," she said. "You can come out now."

And he did, appearing right in front of her not more than five inches away, and she found herself suddenly staring at his smiling mouth.

"Oh, God," Tess moaned. Her knees went suddenly weak and she stepped back to sit heavily on the couch, staring at the man. "Oh, my God."

"I'm still not dressed, lass," he said. The hallway light picked out his shadow.

"I think I believe you," she said. "You're really a dead man?"

"Yes, I'm afraid that I am."

"But how did you come to be here? Why?"

"I have not the faintest idea. I heard you splashing about and went to help you. You can imagine my surprise when I was actually able to grab hold."

"Do you mean you've tried before? You've been up here—up in the world—before?"

"Yes, many times, but never to shore and nobody ever sees or hears me. I have never been able to make contact at all."

"You'll have to tell me the whole story," Tess said then. "This is so strange I can hardly grasp it." Or else the trauma of seeing Darrell had unhinged her.

"I wish I could cover myself first," he said. "I'm not normally a modest man, but you're neither my mother nor a lady of the evening, so I'd like to be a gentleman if I can."

"How can you wear clothes when you can't touch a chair?"

"I don't know as I can."

Tess stood. "You know, if you can touch me, maybe you can touch my clothing, too. I'm afraid I'm smaller than you, but I've got some sweatpants that might not look too horrible. Just a second.''

She ran to her bedroom feeling nearly giddy about the whole thing. She'd either gone crazy or she had a ghost standing in her living room! A naked ghost! It was too outrageous to be believed, and yet it was also too good to be true.

He was a handsome man after all, and he had rescued her like a knight in shining armor. Rescued her twice, really. Could she be imagining this? Could she have gone off the deep end and made up some masculine fantasy figure?

You're not crazy. You didn't make him up. Tess, you only just got rid of one man. Why on earth would you make up another?

She pulled the sweatpants from her drawer. They were her black ones; she didn't think he'd appreciate wearing the pink. Turning back toward the living room, she caught a glimpse of herself in the long mirror on the back of her bureau. She saw an ordinary-looking woman wearing men's pajamas and a light robe, hardly a feminine sight. No makeup or anything! She couldn't imagine what he must think of modern women!

But that couldn't be helped now; the first impression had already been made. She took the garment out to him feeling glumly certain that he must have found her quite unappealing. Tess held the garment out. "All right, Mr. Dyer, see if you can hold on to these."

He reached out and grasped the sweatpants and then bunched and stretched them happily in his hands. "The first cloth I've held in ages!" he exclaimed. "They'll be tight, to be sure, but it is truly amazing that I have something to wear at all." Gabriel moved into the darkest corner of the room and struggled into the pants. A mild oath escaped his lips when his toe caught the elastic in the cuff. "All right, then," he said. "Let's have some light in the room, shall we?"

Tess switched on the light and regarded the man in front of her.

He was just under six feet tall with a broad chest and thickly muscled arms. The pants were stretched tightly over his muscular hips and legs, and stopped at midcalf. Rather than his appearing ridiculous in them, the inherent confidence of his stance allowed him to sport a rather dashing look.

His hands were strong and callused, but with long, artistic fingers like the hands of a piano player. His face was just as she remembered it from the night before. A square-cut study in manly confidence, it bore a small scar on the ridge of his left cheekbone and another on the jaw below it. His lips were wide and full, ready for smiling, and the teeth were surprisingly white and even. The eyes set beneath thick, expressive brows were a lively shade of green that sparkled with his smile. His hair, a dark auburn shade, was long and pulled back into a ponytail with a piece of red ribbon.

Tess just stared at him while he did his best to adjust the pants to his body. What on earth had brought him here? And now that he was here, what on earth was she supposed to do with him?

Gabriel looked up and smiled. "Very comfortable fabric," he said. "We'da earned a pretty penny for cloth such as this in any port of call."

She still couldn't quite believe this was happening. "Is that what you did? You were a merchant seaman?" Tess dropped onto the couch. The evening had been tiring so far, and she could see that it was going to be a long one.

"Well, I suppose you could say I was that."

He looked at the reclining chair behind which he'd been hiding earlier, and then, smoothing his hand down over his newly clad legs, he tentatively lowered himself into it. It supported him perfectly.

"Well, now," he said as he leaned back in the chair, "I guess—" But he didn't finish the sentence. Instead of resting his back against the chair, he fell straight through it and hit the floor with a resounding *thump!* "God's blood!" he shouted in surprise, lying with his hips and legs on the chair and his torso on the floor behind it. When he tried to roll over, his legs hit the arms of the chair and stopped him so that he had to push himself straight up to sit again. "What kind of a world is this where I can wear your trousers but I can't sit in a chair?" he asked her. "I'm at loss here, lass."

Taken aback by his predicament, Tess had also been a bit amused, and she was at a loss to explain it, too. But then she knew, or thought she knew, what had happened.

"Here," she said, rising. "Put this around your shoulders and then sit down again."

She took her robe off and handed it to him as he stood.

"I don't know how I'll look in it," he said, laughing, "but I'll wear it if it pleases you."

"It does," she told him. "Just slip it over your shoulders and try sitting again."

She watched with keen interest to see if her theory would be proven correct. The man lowered himself into the seat and then, very carefully, rested his back against the chair.

"You are most clearly a genius!" he cried out. "Yes, definitely that, for I don't understand it at all."

"Me neither, really," she admitted. "But since you can wear my clothing, it appears that the cloth will act as a buffer between you and the real world."

"A buffer, you say?" He gave it some thought and tested her theory by trying to rest his bare hand on the arm of the chair. His hand passed through the material, disappearing to the wrist. "But if I can touch your clothing, and yourself, as well, why not your furniture?"

"It's not mine," she said. "It's rented."

"Rented? The house, too?"

"Yes, all of it," she admitted.

"That does make fair sense," he said. "But then, how am I able to stand upon this rented floor of yours?"

Tess paused, considering. "I don't know," she confessed.

But he was smiling then, comprehension growing in his lively green eyes. "It's because of you," he said. "The flooring has borne your tread, felt the sole of your foot upon it. Yes, lass, it has the touch of your body upon it and so I can touch it, too. Ah, there's a kinship at work here—your body to mine.''

Tess felt herself blushing. The lilting manner in which he'd said that simple sentence had given it a carnal sound. The touch of my body, she thought, smiling. It was as though her body were a magical charm that could give him form with its touch.

''I don't see why that should be the case,'' she said carefully. ''Why me?''

''Why not you?'' He stretched back against the reclining chair, which immediately responded by unfolding beneath him. ''Oh, saints above, now the chair itself is doing it to me,'' he said. But he laughed, enjoying his reclining position. ''So how does a body get itself up again from this miracle chair?''

''You just grab the arms and pull...no, I guess you can't do that. Here, I'll help.''

Tess hurried to help the man whose hands could not grip the arms of the chair and whose feet made no contact with the extended footrest. She took his hands in hers and pulled, and the chair folded obediently as he rose to stand, her robe falling away from his shoulders. He stood inches before her, still holding both of her hands in his, and smiled down at her.

''I can see where I shall be surprised quite often in this world of yours,'' he said. ''But with you guiding me, I am certain I shall be as safe as a babe in it.''

Then he lifted both of her hands to his mouth and kissed them, a delicate brushing of his lips, first on one hand and then the other.

Tess found herself looking into his wonderfully green eyes and wishing he were more substantial, wishing he could actually be a man she could rely on. But how could a woman possibly rely on a ghost?

"Well," she began, trying to ignore the embarrassment and sudden emotion caused by his kiss. "Well, now that we know a little more about how you can get around in the world, we'll have to figure out how you got here to begin with."

"I'm here," he said, still holding her hands. "Isn't that enough?"

Once again, she felt out of kilter. Had her run-in with Darrell and her unfounded suspicions of Charles Dumont pushed her over the edge—into a world of fantasy? "But we don't know why or how long you'll stay."

"I think I'll stay forever," he told her. "Forever and a day."

"Please, Gabriel," she said, trying to effect a businesslike tone. "Tell me what happened to you. Tell me your story."

"That I will, lass, and gladly. I don't think it will explain my state, but if it will keep you at my side longer, the tale will be well worth the telling."

"I'd love to hear all of it."

"Well, then, I would suppose it best to begin by being as honest as I know how," Gabriel said. "I agreed I was a merchant seaman, which I was to be sure, but our form of commerce wasn't of the type you're thinking, lass. At the time I met my demise, I was making my way in the world as a pirate, you see. In fact, I was captain of the ship."

Tess could think of no reply to that information but to stare at him in wonder. Not only did she have a ghost in her house, but the ghost was a buccaneer!

DARRELL CAGE LEFT TESS'S bungalow nursing his shoulder and looking for a drink. The cellular phone in his car had been ringing when he got to it, however, and he snatched the receiver from its cradle and snarled into it, "Hello, Darrell Cage."

"Are we set, then?" a man asked calmly, ignoring Darrell's obvious ill-temper.

"Almost." Darrell swallowed and took a deep breath as he gazed back in the direction of Teresa's house. "She hasn't signed it yet."

"Why not? We have to break ground in two weeks and we haven't had a title search yet."

"It's tough to get her to sign over property that she doesn't know she owns, Carl. I've got to figure out a plan. But I'll get it. Don't worry."

"You better."

"I saved you millions," Darrell snapped. "Don't lose any sleep over it."

"I won't," Carl assured him. "I'm not the one with his neck on the line. Face it, we'd be better off dealing with her directly...and leaving you out of it completely."

"Then do that and get off my back! Goodbye." Darrell put down the phone, his teeth set in an angry grimace. Between his business "partners" and his ex-wife, he felt as though the whole world had designated him as its target.

He really needed a drink now.

Because it was Sunday, and he didn't want to go to a restaurant, he had to settle for a six-pack of beer from a Qwik-Mart to soothe his aching body.

When Darrell Cage began branching out from his real-estate business into other ventures, he'd found some convenient loopholes that had saved him a lot of expense and red tape. One was to place property in his wife's name to separate it from his business and, in some cases, conceal the ownership. Tess wasn't stupid, of course, and she was an accountant, so she had a pretty good idea of what he was up to when he had her sign various papers. Not that she had any concrete proof that he knew of.

But those papers were the main lever she'd used to obtain the divorce. The only way he'd been able to regain control of the property had been to let it go through uncontested. But she'd been true to her word and signed everything back to him. Everything but one particular piece of property, the deed to which he'd passed off as a duplicate of another to gain her signature.

That remaining signature was his goal now, but every time he saw her he became so angry that he couldn't concentrate. He really didn't care about business papers or signatures, only about her absence from his home. That, and the fact that she had physically ejected him from the rattrap she was now living in. How on earth could that woman throw him out of the place like that?

He drank and nursed his anger, then he drove back toward Tess's house. Maybe he'd stop again and ask her what she thought she was doing manhandling him like that.

Maybe he should tell her how she got her current job. Did she really think a woman seven years out of college with no employment record deserved as good as what she had? He ought to tell her.

No, he ought to belt her. That's what he should do. How dare she twist his arm like that?

When Darrell stopped two houses down from hers, the front tire of his car rode up on the curb. He parked at a cockeyed angle that mirrored his state of mind. He staggered out of his car and swung the door shut, not quite managing to close it. The dome light of his vehicle remained on.

As Darrell walked toward the lights glowing in Tess's windows, a shadow moved across the shade. Something gave him the impression that she wasn't alone.

That thought made him angrier still.

He stalked closer to the house, never seeing the other car parked at the curb in front of his. He would have recognized the car; he'd seen it before. But Darrell was too drunk and too angry.

He sneaked through the yard to a side window and peered through the slim space between the sill and the drawn shade. He could see Tess's back and could hear her talking, but he couldn't see anyone else in the room.

Hoping to find a better vantage point, Darrell moved around the house toward the small backyard, stumbling over something in the dark.

"Damn," he muttered as he regained his footing. Then, in the brief silence following his oath, he heard a footstep.

A man loomed in front of him, blocking his way.

"You?" Darrell spoke angrily, but in a whisper. "I thought you were... Hey! What are you doing out here?"

The man came at him quickly, his arm slamming into Darrell's stomach, knocking him down.

Darrell let out a small yelp of pain, clutched his stomach and tried to roll away from the man. But the dark form stooped over him, his arm striking Darrell repeatedly until he lay quite still.

Then, after pausing a moment to catch his breath, the man took Darrell's inert body by the ankles and dragged it across the lawn toward the garage, leaving a trail of bent grass behind him.

Chapter Five

"What was that?" Tess sat up abruptly on the couch. She turned toward the back of the house as she strained to hear. She'd *thought* she'd heard something.

"I heard nothing." Gabriel followed her gaze toward the kitchen, a look of concern darkening his brow. "Would you wish me to see about it for you?"

"No," she said, shaking her head in dismissal. "It's probably just the wind. I'd rather hear about your life. You said you were in Africa. What were you trading there?"

"We had stopped an English merchant ship on the West Africa route," he said, regaining the momentum of his story. "She was loaded with muskets and gunpowder for an outpost to the south, but we redirected the shipment to a French garrison in Guinea, where they weren't too particular about the source of their supply. I led a group inland looking for ivory or anything upon which we might lay claim and earn a profit."

"What did you do with the crew of the ship you captured?"

"Set them that didn't join us adrift in the ship's boat," he said easily. Then, noting her frown, he added, "They were within sight of shore at the time, lass, and all of them were fit for rowing. And nearly half the crew elected to stay aboard and pilot the ship to port for us. Merchant crews held little loyalty to the ship's masters, and they did well for themselves in the sale of the supplies and the ship, as well. Can you find fault with that arrangement?"

"It's hard to get used to conversing with a pirate's ghost, I guess," Tess said. "Your concept of fairness is quite different from mine. The arrangement seems brutal."

"That it was," he agreed. "But life in Dublin or London was no less brutal for the majority of the poor sinners whom the good Lord put down there. Survival was our game no matter where we were, and it was no different for the men of the ships we captured in our brief career."

"I suppose not. What about going inland? I didn't think pirates did anything but attack ships at sea."

"A pirate is a man of business working beyond the legal pale," Gabriel said with a twinkle in his eye. "Instead of buying and selling, we stole and sold. It brings a greater profit."

"I see you're an unrepentant pirate at that."

"I have no reason to repent," he insisted. "The list of my sins may be long, but I'd set it against that of any king or nobleman of my day and come out a saint in comparison. And now that I'm back, more or less," he added, laughing, "God has apparently given me a chance to make my list a bit longer."

"Well, I hope that's not your plan." Tess frowned. "How did you get started? I don't imagine the Pirates' Guild recruited new members on the street."

"No, the British did that for them," he said bitterly. "I was convicted of theft and condemned to transportation to New South Wales but I slipped away from a work detail and took my own route off the island on a Dutch ship. I was sixteen at the time, you understand, and I'd have sooner been shot dead escaping than forced into servitude.

"Well, the Dutch trader stopped in the Lesser Antilles and I jumped ship. I made it to Jamaica, where I settled down in a way. I married a fine woman—Camille, her name was. The most beautiful lass you might hope to see. I'd thought I'd found heaven, you understand, in the glance of Camille's eyes. It's her ribbon that binds my hair even now."

"But you left her?"

"She died, miss. Cholera is a fancy word for death, and she succumbed to the scourge in the plague of 1636."

"I'm sorry," Tess said. "It must have been terrible for you."

"No finer woman ever lived," he said simply. "But life was brutal, as I say. Death was not something that surprised anyone. I set sail a month after putting her in the ground. Our ship was taken by the crew of the *Maria Louisa* no more than two months later."

"And you joined them?"

"Certainly. What else did I have to do with my life? I wasn't going to work for sailor's pay until I was too crippled to work and left to die a beggar in some foreign port of call. No, I'd run my own life or ruin it, but I wouldn't let some bloody bastard of a ship's master run it to ruin for me. Excuse my language,'' he added quickly. "I'm a bit rusty in my etiquette."

"That's all right," Tess assured him. "Those words are vulgar, but they're not usually considered to be quite as terribly offensive anymore."

"Well, things have changed to be sure when women wear pants and sailors are allowed to curse in public," he said, marveling. "But I imagine I'll get used to it."

"You were going to tell me about Africa," Tess said. "Did you find ivory?"

"Not much," he replied. "We weren't equipped to hunt the brutes and could only trade a little with the native tribes. I was the only one who made a profit on that jaunt or could have had I ever put to a port where I might have sold my prize."

"What was that?"

"It was an amulet of sorts," Gabriel said. "It was carved from a hardwood I hadn't seen, almost the size of a man's fist. The face of it was inlaid with ivory and gold fetishes and a red stone the size of my thumb was in the center of the design. It was a fine piece of jewelry, and the owner parted with it for nothing at all."

"Nothing?"

"Yes, he said it was good luck to give it away. The translation was poor, you understand, but I was given to believe it was a magic charm."

"But he still gave it to you?"

"I suppose he felt he needed the luck, for he was nearly wasted away with fever when I found him. He was a traveler, not one of the tribe with whom we found him staying. Poor fellow was alone and away from his home and he wanted to buy himself a bit of luck by giving away his charm."

"You were planning to sell it?"

"Certainly, miss. I don't know the type of stone that was in it—a ruby, I would imagine, though it was darker than I'd seen before—but it would have been worth a great deal in Amsterdam were I to ever get there."

"You never did."

"No, we were surprised by British men-of-war and had to make way in a grand hurry. We left our captain hopping and spitting on the coast of Africa." Gabriel laughed at the memory. "A foul man. No one missed him. I was his first mate, and so I took command."

"Were you the one who gave the order to set sail, too?"

"That I was," he admitted. "But then, as I say, there was no love lost between the crew and him. They all put their backs to the task of sailing readily enough when I gave the order. We split the treasures in his cabin equally among us."

"But they turned on you just as quickly as they had on him," Tess said. "Why?"

"They said I had cursed them. The superstitious heathen accused me of jinxing the voyage with my African witchery. The amulet, you see. They could all see its value and wanted it for that, but they were afraid of it, too.

"The voyage did seem cursed," he continued. "We made landfall in the Bahamas in mid-July but the British were there . . . a lovely little welcoming committee when we arrived. Of course, they couldn't know about the ship in Africa, but we had reputation enough in Caribbean waters to give them cause to fire on us. We fought gamely, and God was kind enough to allow for a misty night in which we could slip away."

Tess sat enthralled by the tale this man had to tell. He'd traveled the world and fought for his place in it, and now he'd come to an underfurnished bungalow to tell his story to a woman three hundred and fifty years after his death. How this miracle had come to pass, and why, was beyond any reason. But the longer he talked, the more she was sure it wasn't her imagination.

"What happened then?"

"We finally put on provisions in Haiti in August," he said. "But the storm season was on us then. We wanted to find a port in which to hide, but the fleet was ever in our wake. We set sail again, landing at Jamaica and then running north through the Yucatán Channel past Cuba and on to America where fate dealt us a cruel blow.

"We thought to be sheltered by the peninsula, you see, but a hurricane curled up behind us, driving us toward shore just at the point where you were swimming the other night. I'll admit, it did seem that the storm was following us, but to say it was my doing was foolishness pure and simple. Yet that's what they did.

"I think it was my booty they really wanted," he said knowingly. "They accused me of taking a greater share of the spoils since assuming my first mate's duties. Incidentally, that wasn't true. Cheating a shipmate was a good way to get killed. I resented the implication, and told them so, but they persisted, saying I was a cheat and a Jonah and they'd have a look in my kit to make certain. I'd have none of that, and told them I'd sooner throw my booty overboard then let them paw through it."

Gabriel paused, reflecting, and then said, "I think now that it was probably a foolish thing, what I did. I was angry and not thinking right. I just threw the leather satchel in which I'd kept my share over the years right over the side of the ship."

"You threw your money over?" Tess was shocked and confused. It seemed that the point of everything had been to gain money, yet he threw his away on a point of honor among thieves. "Why?"

"I could read the storm well enough to know we wouldn't be long on the surface," he explained. "I couldn't swim a stroke, myself, and surely wouldn't have gotten far with a bag of gold in my hand. No, I threw it away just to make them cry for it. I think now it probably made me look the more guilty that I wouldn't let them see what was inside the bag. I should have handed it to them and thrown my fancy amulet over instead. But they angered me, and I don't think too well when angered."

"That's when you went over the side?" Tess asked.

"Yes, immediately after my gold. I went down like a rock and never even bobbed to the surface. It's not really so bad a way to go compared to some ways I've seen people die."

"What about your ship?"

"Thirty miles due north of my bones lies the wreck of the *Maria Louisa,*" he said quietly. "She went down with all hands and all her stores and fittings, and every man of the crew took his gold down with him."

"It must be worth millions now."

"Aye, I suppose that it would," he agreed. "If a fellow knew where to look, he could have a king's ransom."

He didn't need to point out that he knew where to look; his broad grin said that quite eloquently.

TESS ONLY WENT TO BED that night because she couldn't avoid it. She had no desire to quit talking to Gabriel. She kept looking for some magician's trick to give him away as an imposter, but every word the man said, every movement he made, proclaimed that he was telling the truth. From his accent and quaint manner of speech to the rolling way he walked, he was what he said he was—a sailor from the era of mainsails and mizzenmasts.

Besides, there was no earthly reason for anyone to want to convince her that he was a seventeenth-century ghost.

The possible reason for his presence was unclear, however, as was any explanation as to how he came to return. But it seemed to Tess that none of that made any difference since he was obviously here regardless of the cause.

She had to admit to herself that she did harbor a small wish that he had returned in order to retrieve his pirated gold. She could well imagine the bounty of the ship that still lay buried in the sand beneath the gulf off the coast of Florida. He would obviously need a living partner to help bring it up, wouldn't he?

The vision of gold doubloons and sparkling jewels shimmered just beyond reach as sleep claimed her that night. Gold doubloons and Gabriel's wonderful green eyes . . .

AFTER TESS WENT TO BED, Gabriel experimented with this new physical world for a while. He wasn't tired, hadn't been for over three hundred years, and he was just as perplexed by his circumstances as Tess was.

He tried picking things up—books, small bowls, various other objects—all without success. He found that he could grasp Tess's coat and a glass from which she drank, but not her books and writing implements. This puzzled him for a moment. She had obviously touched the books and printed matter, or else they wouldn't be in the house. They must be hers by right of ownership. Why couldn't he touch them, as well?

Then he knew. She had had intimate contact with the coat by wearing it, and the glass had felt the touch of her lips on its rim. The thought of her lovely lips touching the glass made him smile.

It was the intimate contact that made the difference. He put his hand on the ribbon that held his hair in confirmation of that thought.

His dear Camille had tied the strip of red ribbon around his hair as a gentleman's adornment when his hair was only at his shoulders. She had taken the ribbon from her dress. Though he hadn't worn it exclusively over the years, he had kept it and used it often when his hair wasn't cut short or braided. It was Camille's ribbon, and after her death, it was all he had besides her memory.

Still touching the ribbon, Gabriel looked toward Tess's door, wondering why her contact should be as strong as his departed wife's had been. She was a beautiful woman, that was true, but he hadn't known anything about her before the sounds of her floundering in the sea brought him to her rescue. He hadn't really expected to be able to touch her any more than he'd been able to touch other swimmers who'd come near his resting place. He'd expected to watch her drown, yet he'd gone to her rescue, hoping things would be different.

When he had actually been able to help her, he had been pleasantly surprised. And, when he carried her to land and she opened her eyes to look at him, he had felt a surge in his heart that he hadn't felt in ages. Perhaps he'd never felt that surge except . . . except with Camille.

Gabriel walked to Tess's door and reached for the knob. His hand slipped through it as though it was nothing more than a shadow in the mist. He smiled wryly. A rented house. Then he shrugged and walked through the equally insubstantial wall.

He was stopped abruptly, his torso and arms snapping forward into Tess's room and then out again. He stepped back in wonder. Why on earth...? Of course. He was wearing her trousers and they were not designed to pass through solid matter.

Thinking that it was a foolish whim to want to look at her, he returned to the couch and sat idly waving his hand to and fro through the arm of it. Then he slapped his palms on his knees, enjoying the solid feeling of their impact and the *thwack* of sound that went through the air.

It might not be gentlemanly, but he just had to have another look at the face he'd carried up from the deep. Gabriel stood resolutely and stripped off the sweatpants and then walked through her wall.

He stopped just inside the dark room and waited to see if she had noticed his arrival. She didn't stir, but continued lying on her back and breathing with the slow rhythm of peaceful sleep.

Gabriel approached her bed now, his gaze focused on her face. Though her eyes were shut, the lids flickered now and then with her dreams, and her lips pursed slightly with each outward breath. She was a fine woman, that was evident. And he remembered the look of honesty and forthrightness that shone in her eyes when they were open. Surely, a beautiful woman.

He could feel again the surging of blood in his veins as he watched her sleep. He knew then that he wanted to always be there to protect her and watch over her.

Perhaps she needed his help, and that was why he was allowed the grace to touch her. But perhaps *he* needed her help. Or maybe the need was mutual. He sighed. Maybe there was no real reason for his presence here. He was just here and that was all there was to it.

Teresa Miller, he thought. It was an English name, but he had the feeling that she didn't hold any special feeling for England. No, he thought now, she explained that she's American. Besides, there was no real harm in her being English. No, even if she were as English as a tankard of ale, he wouldn't care.

She shifted in her sleep, pushing away the sheet that covered her on this warm night. Gabriel noticed then that the first three buttons of her cotton top were unbuttoned. When she changed position on the bed, pushing her covers away, he could see her left breast in the gentle moonlight with the darker flesh of her nipple blending into the shadow beneath her garment.

Gabriel tried to be a gentleman and look away; he had no business in her room to begin with after all. But he couldn't force his eyes to move. He knew that if he chose to reach down right now, he could kiss her, as well. He could . . .

No, he could not. Gabriel stepped away and backed through the wall to the safety of the darkened living room, his heart pounding. And, though he had neither heart nor blood in his insubstantial veins, he felt himself turning crimson.

Was this his punishment for leading a pirate's life? No more fiendish punishment could ever be devised! In this day and age, he could follow his most base instincts with a woman without fear of retribution, but he was of such a mind that he could never do such a thing. By the standards of the social system in which he'd grown, Gabriel Dyer was no gentleman, but by any other standard he was.

Well, if this was his punishment, he would make the best of it.

He chuckled quietly now. Tess would probably think him odd to have willingly killed men in his time, yet blanch at the idea of kissing a sleeping woman, catching her unaware. He slipped into the sweat-pants again and sat on the couch. After a moment, he stood, feeling restive in his new surroundings. He felt, well, he supposed that he felt a bit hungry. The feeling bothered him, for he hadn't been hungry in all his years beneath the waves. Neither hunger nor sleep had assailed him, but he was definitely hungry now.

Of course, there was the small problem of feeding himself since he didn't suppose he would be able to touch any of the food in her larder. He didn't even know where she stored her food. He had heard mention of a kitchen, however, and he remembered what door she'd come through earlier with her glass of juice. He walked into that room and looked around him.

It was harder to see in this room. Its one window was shaded from the moonlight by a tree in her yard. His eyes landed on a square metal thing painted white. There were many cupboards, too, all closed, and a tall white item matching what he now assumed was the stove. It looked to be only a big box with two doors. Perhaps she kept her fresh food in there. He'd have to find a way to open it.

He remembered that there had been a scarf in the pocket of her coat. If he was able to touch the coat, he could surely touch the scarf. That, in turn, could be used to open the door of the mysterious box.

Gabriel hurried back to the living room and returned with the scarf. He was about to slip the scarf through the handle of the white box when a sound behind him stopped his movements. He turned slowly. A man was looking through the window of the back door!

Gabriel froze, ready to repel the intruder but unsure whether Tess knew the man or not. And could the man see him? Apparently not. He set to work, trying to unlock the door.

If he was having this much difficulty, then he couldn't have a key, so Gabriel concluded that he was no friend of the household. He stepped to the side and stood ready. The man finally opened the door and peered into the dark house. He took a step inside, pausing to listen, and Gabriel swung his fist at him with all his might.

But his fist flew unseen through the intruder's face, and Gabriel stifled a curse at his stupidity.

The man seemed to notice something wrong, however. He cocked his head as though sniffing the air for trouble. He took another step. As he lifted one gloved hand, something in it gleamed.

Gabriel kicked out his covered leg, catching the man at knee level. The man jumped back, startled by the unseen block to his movement. When he looked to see what had stopped him, Gabriel hit him with his fist, which he'd wrapped with Tess's scarf.

The man flew back through the door, landing on his rear end on the flagstone patio. He stared without comprehension into the house. Then he bolted to his feet and ran from the yard, with the sound of Gabriel's laughter giving speed to his feet.

"I don't know what business you thought you had here," Gabriel said aloud, "but you'd be better served to do your calling in daylight from now on."

Then, pleased with his work, Gabriel used his knee to push the door shut against future intruders.

Chapter Six

"You had a caller last night, lass."

"What?" When Tess came into her kitchen, she found Gabriel seated on the floor. He was unsuccessfully trying to eat an apple, which he held with the aid of her good scarf. She frowned, not expecting his first words to concern company at her door.

"A burglar, I would assume." Gabriel stood and rather reverently placed the apple on the countertop. "He managed to open your kitchen door, but I sent him packing."

"Maybe I missed something here," she said, "but are you telling me that someone tried to break into my house last night, you stopped him, and then you didn't tell me about it?"

"That's the size of it, to be sure," he said. "I didn't see where I should disturb your sleep when the miscreant was well on his way. It was too dark to tell, but I would imagine it was that fellow who assaulted you earlier, miss, and so he was basically harmless."

"Yes, Darrell would try breaking in, wouldn't he?" she mused.

"That was my assumption, lass."

"Gabriel," Tess said, scratching her head tiredly, "let's get one thing straight right away. My name is Teresa, or Tess, so you don't have to call me miss, and for God's sake, don't call me lass. Calling a grown woman lass could land you in a heap of trouble in some quarters."

"I'll take that point to heart," he said.

"Now what about this burglar?" Tess filled her coffeemaker as he told her what had happened, aching for her first cup of coffee.

"How did you manage to hit the man?" she asked as she sat at the table, waiting for the coffee to brew.

"I made use of your scarf," he said, smiling. He wrapped the scarf around his hand to demonstrate. "I couldn't have hit him tremendously hard, however, for I see I didn't bloody the cloth."

"Good thing you didn't. That's my good one." She yawned, wondering if she could afford to call in sick today. "I can't see why anyone would break into my house. I don't have anything of value, that's for sure."

"You've got yourself," he said earnestly. "And I don't suppose people have changed so greatly in the past three hundred years that some men wouldn't break down a door to get at you."

Tess smiled at the roundabout compliment. Except for Charles Dumont, it had been a while since a man had expressed thoughts of that kind about her.

"I wish you would have woken me up," she said. "We could have called the police."

"Police? Do you mean the law now? Lord, girl, why would you want them interfering in your affairs?"

"Gabriel, don't call me girl, either. Okay?"

"I'm confused by your language. Bastard is fitting enough to say, but girl has become a bad word." He shook his head in wonderment.

"It's not a bad word," she said, rubbing her eyes. "But I'm twenty-nine years old. I'm not a girl. I'm a woman. Fully developed and everything."

"Well, I can see that much," he said. "It's the word I wonder about."

Tess could see him reddening beneath his saltwater tan, and marveled at finding a man who could blush. "Calling a woman a girl is seen as an insult, that's all. What if I called you boy?"

"If you were my mother, I wouldn't mind. And if you were of the upper class, I'd expect it," he said, nodding. "And so I see what you mean, for I surely wouldn't like it coming from the likes of them."

"Right. So, when you say girl, it implies you think you're better than the woman you're talking to," Tess said. "I guarantee she won't like it. Of course, I realize you come from a different time and country. You were raised to think of women as inferior, I suppose."

"Now who gave you that impression?" he exclaimed. "Is that something they teach in books these days? That we thought of our women as inferior?"

"*Our* women?" She arched an eyebrow. "Well, yes."

"Physically, of course. I could whip you with my good arm tied behind me, and you can't deny that. But no one can outthink a woman, and any man could tell you as much. It wouldn't have been natural for the good Lord to have made women with lesser strength and not given them the intelligence to avoid a fight. And what of the household? My mother ran the house for eight children and my father drunk half the time. She kept us clothed and fed on an amount of money an English noble wouldn't stoop to pick up from the street. My father could earn the money with the sweat of his brow, but he couldn't keep hold of it without my mother. He'da drunk all of it up if not for her."

"Okay, I stand corrected," Tess said, laughing. "You seem to have a strong opinion on the matter."

"I don't like to be thought of as a heathen," he said. "No more, I suppose, than you want to be thought of as a girl. The word is just a means of address for me. And, in the days I come from, when hard work stole the youth from everybody, calling a woman a girl was a compliment. It had nothing to do with inferiority."

"I guess I've seen too many pirate movies," Tess said. She rose to fill her coffee cup. "In the movies, the guys run around having sword fights and carousing with . . . well . . . whores."

"Of course there was some of that," he admitted. "I don't imagine there is much dueling going on these days, but is prostitution not allowed now, either?"

"Of course not."

"Well, it's a shame a woman isn't allowed to earn a living by whatever means she might choose," he said. "Most likely the clergy made that rule."

"They influenced it, I'm sure. But it's hardly a decent profession!"

"No, perhaps not." He frowned. "I have the impression that women fill a great many jobs these days."

"They do." Tess smiled. "Now, what on earth were you doing with that apple?"

"Oh, it was a sorry state you found me in," he said. "I'm feeling every year since I last ate a meal, Tess."

"I can't think how you'll manage to do anything about your hunger," Tess said.

"Nor can I," Gabriel admitted. "I've been fighting with that piece of fruit all the night long only to prove to myself that I'm incapable of eating it."

"Tell me something," she said as she slipped two pieces of bread into her toaster and pushed the lever down, "what did you do all the time you were, you know, under the gulf?"

"It was like I was half-asleep, not fully aware, and just drifting on the tide for the most part. Sometimes I'd be fully awake and have a look about me, but mostly it was like a long and dreary dream," he said absently as he looked at the toaster. "Pardon me, but I've noticed that you managed to make a fine jug of coffee in no time at all. And now, if I'm not mistaken, you're toasting bread for yourself. How is that possible?"

"I've got an electric coffeemaker," she said. "And the toaster is electric, too."

"Electric?"

"Yes, well, that's something they've come up with since you were here last. I don't know how to explain it quickly except to say that there's a bunch of receptacles around the place. There." She pointed at the wall socket above the counter where the toaster was plugged in. "There's power in each of those, and when we plug something in, the power goes into it, too."

"And I take it that this power turns into heat to brew the coffee and toast your bread," he said.

"Right. Just like with the lights."

"Ah, so that explains the mystery of your household lighting," Gabriel said with a broad smile. "I was going to ask that last night, but thought I'd look foolish asking."

"You could never look foolish," Tess said. "Not you."

"So that's the cause of the remarkable cold within your small pantry, too?"

"What? Oh, the refrigerator. Yes, that's electric, too. Be careful not to get any electrical appliance wet, okay?"

"And why would that be?"

"You can get a nasty shock. It could even kill you. Well, not you," she said, laughing. "But it can kill most people."

"I'll bear that in mind."

Tess's toast popped up and she buttered it quickly and applied a thin layer of apple jelly. "None of this helps you get something to eat, though, does it?"

"No, that it doesn't."

She took a bite of toast and then paused, looking at the man's hungry eyes on her food. "Were you ever hungry...down there?"

"No, not a whit."

"Never sleepy? Or cold?"

"Neither," he admitted.

"What if you went back?"

"Do you want to be rid of me?"

"No, not that. But I was thinking that you might go back, or turn invisible, or something. Then you might get rid of your hunger."

"That is possible, I would think. But I'm not entirely certain how to get back."

"You can walk away just like you did on the beach," she suggested.

"I tried to leave your house last night thinking I might find edible fare outside," Gabriel said. "But I couldn't get out the door."

Tess scrubbed her fingers back through her hair, looking down at her toast hungrily. She had to get ready for work soon. "Well, try to describe what happened the other night again."

"I heard you splashing in the surf," he said. "And, as I had on many occasions, I went toward the sound thinking I might be of assistance. Normally, I'm as good as not there. This time, however, I reached out and actually grabbed ahold of you."

"And carried me to shore."

"Exactly."

"Then what? You went away, and I didn't see you until you showed up last night. Where did you go?"

"Into the water." He shrugged. "Beyond that, I don't know. Except, of course, that I thought of you and wondered how it was that I was allowed to touch you. I wondered if I could ever find out where you lived so that I might, well, see you again."

"And how did you manage to find me?"

"You called my name," he said. "I fairly flew to your side at the sound of it."

"I called, and you came running."

"Yes, but I'd be a liar to say it was voluntary. Not that I would have tarried," he added quickly. "But I was suddenly transported here."

"Just like a fairy godfather," Tess said.

"Oh, I'd be glad to be that for you," he said earnestly. "If only that much."

"I was sure glad to have your help. Wait! You walked away from me and returned to the ocean. What if I go to work and drive away from you? Do you think you might go back to the way you were again?"

"Thereby alleviating my hunger without benefit of food," Gabriel concluded.

"Right. Do you think it will work?" Tess asked eagerly.

"It might at that," he agreed.

"Great, then I'll just get ready for work and be on my way," she said. "Then you won't be hungry."

"If you could do that for me, I'd surely be grateful. And, in the meantime, you would be well advised to finish your meal." He pointed at her cold toast. "Don't starve yourself in sympathy for my hunger. I didn't pull you from the ocean for that."

TESS HAD TO HURRY. Her conversation with Gabriel had taken time she ordinarily spent dressing and so she was in a rush.

As she blew her hair dry and buttoned her blouse in front of the mirror, she shuddered at the thought of how she'd come out to the kitchen this morning. Pajama clad and rubbing the sleep from her eyes, she had been a sight, with not a hint of makeup and her hair a mess.

He hadn't seemed to notice, however. The way his eyes had stayed on her hadn't shown anything but the deepest interest and the clear glow of desire. Or she'd been seeing more than was there. Maybe the light in his eyes was there simply because she was the only woman on Earth whom he could touch.

She'd better keep on her toes with this man. He seemed to be a gentleman, but the fact was that he'd been without a woman for a very long time. Just as his appetite for food had come back to him now, other desires might overpower him, as well.

But Tess had no time to worry. Besides, this morning, leaving the house might be a mission of mercy.

AT TEN MINUTES before nine, when Tess left the house, Gabriel experienced a tugging in his chest. It was as if his heart were connected by some kind of invisible thread to Tess. He watched her strange metal-and-glass vehicle pull away rapidly, without benefit of horses to draw it along the road.

He felt his hunger increase rather than decrease. Then, suddenly, echoing the distance she was so rapidly putting between them, the hunger started to fade until it was entirely gone.

He stood in her living room wondering what would happen next. It appeared that nothing was going to happen at all. Then, as though in answer to his unspoken question, the trousers he wore fell away. They slipped through his legs and landed in a heap on the floor.

His shadow, a feeble darkening on the floor in the morning light, disappeared entirely, though he could still see himself. Then he lost contact with the floor and began drifting through the house. But he didn't return to his watery grave.

Instead, he moved through the rear of the house, passing out over the flagstone patio to look at the yard. It was outside, in the light of day, that an odd premonition overcame him. He felt something strangely foreign in the yard.

A path of bent grass stretched across the small yard toward a building in the back. Yes, and the path was discolored, darkened slightly. He almost grasped what was odd about it, but the ringing of Tess's doorbell caught his attention.

Gabriel moved through the house again. Two men in dark uniforms were standing on her front step. They wore beaked caps and colored glasses, and shiny badges gleamed on the chests of their dark shirts.

Gabriel didn't need to be told who those ominously garbed strangers might be. An officer of the law needs no introduction, no matter what century it is.

"She's not home," one of the men said.

"We've got her business address," the other younger one said. "We can catch her there."

"Catch her? You sound so eager," the first man said. "We're just calling on the victim's ex-wife for identification. She's not a suspect."

"Not yet. But I'll bet it's her." The young officer laughed as they walked away. "She probably got stiffed on alimony or something."

Apparently, the fellow Tess had thrown from her home the night before had been killed. And, if Gabriel understood constables, Tess would soon be accused of the crime.

Suddenly, his premonition returned. The discoloration on the grass had been... *No, it can't be.* He flew back through the house, plaster and lath blurring past him. Yes, clearly something had been dragged over the lawn, leaving intermittent stains of rusty brown behind.

"I'll be damned entirely to hell if that's not blood," Gabriel said to himself. "The blackguard was killed here as we spoke last night!"

And that meant that the intruder whom he'd turned away had probably been after Tess with the same intention! Now the law was after her, too, and the evidence of the crime was in plain sight.

He had to warn her that she was being stalked by both a vicious murderer and the law! But their plan to separate had worked too well. He had no idea where to find her now!

Chapter Seven

"You're late."

James Bentsen, general manager of Crowe Tool and Die, met her at the door at six minutes after nine. He was in his shirtsleeves, and they were rolled up and his tie loosened a bit at his collar, giving him the appearance of having been at work for hours already. Of course, his normal arrival time was at a quarter of the hour, which gave him enough time to adjust his wardrobe to greet the rest of the staff.

"I'm sorry." She bustled to her desk. "I had some unexpected house guests come in yesterday. I had to get them situated for the day."

"I should think that anyone old enough to arrive unannounced is also old enough to look out for themselves," he snipped. "Don't make a habit of being late, Teresa."

"I won't, Mr. Bentsen."

Thankfully, he left her alone once she'd taken her place at her desk. The man seemed happy she had come in late. It gave him a chance to tell her not to do it again; it was the first opportunity he'd had.

As she watched the officious manager walk away, Tess felt the stirrings of rebellion. It wasn't the job itself that prompted these random feelings of rebellion, for she loved working with numbers. No, it was that man in particular.

She'd been employed at Crowe Tool for just under six months, starting there after a lengthy job search that began when she'd filed papers for divorce. Once she hit the six-month mark, she would qualify for the employee health plan and receive a small raise in pay, both of which she desperately needed. So, she certainly couldn't afford to quit a job that she basically liked just because of Mr. Bentsen, she reminded herself.

Divorce hadn't been easy. Sometimes, she wished she'd asked for alimony. She could have kept her new car rather than having to trade down to the dented old Toyota she was driving now. And she could have avoided bouncing her TV and stereo in and out of the pawnshop for most of the year.

But, after a rocky job search, she was well situated in this position and about to knock a substantial chunk out of her monthly expenses by getting on the health plan. And, though she hadn't used her accounting degree during her marriage to Darrell, she had proven herself capable at her profession. As long as she could learn to ignore people like Bentsen, she'd be fine. When she hit the six-month mark, she'd treat herself to a new dress and an evening out with her friend, Betty Crown, using the money that would have gone to her health premium.

Tess glanced around. Her desk was one of three behind the reception counter in the main office of Crowe Tool. Beside her desk was that of Juanita Hunnicut, the office manager. The receptionist, Barb Davis, was seated in front of them, just behind the high counter. Juanita was on vacation this week, so only Tess and Barb were in the office.

The company officers—James Bentsen, Paul Weatherly, who was vice president and head of sales, and company president, Burton Renfrew—each had his own office.

Tess switched on her computer, letting it run through its opening routine while she took the billing slips from her IN basket and prepared to tally the company's sales from the past week. It was rather routine work, but she hoped this job might become a stepping stone to more money and responsibility at another company.

She thought briefly about Charles Dumont and his offer of employment, but shook that thought away with a wry smile. That offer was heavily laden with implications, none of them very businesslike. Besides, all she really knew about the guy was that he said he was a banker and dressed the part. Until she saw his office, with his name on the door, she wouldn't think about any offers from him.

Now she wished she hadn't accepted his invitation to dinner tomorrow night. At the time, she hadn't expected to ever see Gabriel again, hadn't remembered his name for that matter. Yes, with Gabriel Dyer in the picture, she found herself mentally crossing Charlie Dumont off her dating list.

Compared with Gabriel, no man she knew stood a chance. No man *alive*.

She winced, trying not to wonder what it would be like to make love to a ghost. But they *could* touch each other. In fact, she was the only woman Gabriel could touch, presumably. *How romantic!* The thought of a man dedicated wholly to her, whose touch was meant only for her, was intriguing.

But then the relationship wouldn't be his choice, would it? He would be bound as a servant was bound to a master, loving her because she was the only one he could love. He'd as much as admitted that he'd come to her home last night because her call had transported him, rather than by conscious choice.

A man who wasn't free to leave couldn't commit himself to a woman. And she'd never know if he did love her, then, would she?

Stop thinking about love with a guy who drowned over three hundred years ago and pay attention to your work. Go on your date with Charlie and see what happens. Concentrate on the living.

She could tell herself anything she wanted, but her thoughts strayed back to Gabriel Dyer anyway.

She could still see the gleam of moonlight on his muscular chest, water glistening on his broad shoulders, and feel the touch of his strong hands carrying her to shore. The memory of his lips upon hers lingered, despite efforts to forget, and she found herself wanting to feel them once more. Just the memory of his kiss gave her a tingling glow inside. He was a magnificent man, someone who would always be surrounded by an aura of strength and pride.

Yes, he would always seem different in some intangible way, as if he were more confident than any modern man, more substantial. It was odd to feel that way about him, since he was technically less substantial, but there was a solidity in his demeanor that most men were lacking. Gabriel didn't wait to see what was expected before showing what he was; he was up front with his personality.

Of course, if he were alive, they'd have to do something with the hair. She didn't know any men with hair that long these days, and it made him look like a rock musician....

Tess blinked. She reminded herself that,for the next eight hours, she owed her employer her complete concentration. Unfortunately, when she looked at the green numbers glowing on her screen, all she saw were Gabriel's magnificent green eyes.

"Hey, are you dreaming?"

Tess looked up abruptly to see Betty Crown leaning on the edge of her desk. Betty was in charge of shipping, and she had been instrumental in securing Tess's position for her. Tess had met the energetic blonde at the courthouse. Betty had been waiting to appear in traffic court the day Tess filed her divorce papers.

"Gapped out a minute, I guess," Tess admitted. "Was it that obvious?"

"No, but you looked like a woman busy thinking about a man," Betty said. "I called you last night. Did you have a date?"

"Yes, I did," Tess said.

"The conspicuous lack of a smile seems to say it wasn't much of a date. What's the story?"

"It was all right, but he's not Mr. Right."

"So who is he, and where'd you meet him, and as long as he isn't your Mr. Right, does he like blondes?"

"His name is Charles Dumont, he's a banker, and I met him on the beach near Bernie's," Tess replied. "I don't know if he likes blondes or not."

"Out for a moonlight stroll?"

"No, well, it's a long story." Tess shook her head, remembering how foolish she'd felt yesterday morning. "But the conclusion of the tale is that I'm having dinner with him tomorrow night and I wish I could get out of it."

"Throwing him back so soon? Why?"

"I don't know where to begin, Betty, and I sure can't do it here. Besides, you'd never believe me."

"Well, you've certainly got me interested in hearing all about it now," Betty said. "Busy tonight?"

"Yes. Well, actually, I don't know if I'm busy or not. I'll call you."

"Sounds fair enough." Betty looked around, smiling. "I guess I'd better get back to the loading dock before Bentsen shows up to deliver his speech about chatting on company time. See you later."

"'Bye, Betty."

Tess watched her friend leave, wondering how she could possibly tell her all that had happened since her ocean swim. Could she just come out and say that she'd met a ghost? No, there was no explaining the situation, not even to Betty. She had a hard enough time understanding the situation herself, so how could she ever explain it?

Tess had just resigned herself to settling into a day with Lotus when Barb Davis buzzed her with a phone call. The watch-your-back tone in Barb's voice indicated that it was a personal call.

"Hello. Tess Miller," she said, trapping the receiver between her chin and shoulder as she keystroked.

"Ah, Tess, I found you." Charles Dumont sounded very pleased with himself. "No more than three calls, too. I should have been a detective."

"I'm flattered that you would go to the trouble," she responded, smiling. The man was nothing if not persistent.

"It's well worth the effort," he said. "But I do think I should be rewarded with the opportunity to take you to lunch."

"I had planned to brown-bag it today," she admitted, thinking of her meager lunch of carrots and an apple. "I appreciate the offer, though."

"Not very much, you don't." Charles laughed. "You'd rather eat something from a bag than go out to lunch with me? I'm hurt."

"You'll survive," she said lightly.

"I don't think so. Come on, a quick bite at Molly's won't harm you one bit," he insisted, naming a popular seafood restaurant nearby.

"You seem terribly concerned with my eating habits," Tess said. "As I recall, we have a date for dinner tomorrow evening."

"And you hadn't planned to eat until then?"

"Yes, I, oh, I suppose I can squeeze you into my schedule," she said, relenting because of Molly's seafood platter rather than Charles Dumont's charms.

She saw the policemen enter the office as she spoke. They stopped at the receptionist's desk, talking briefly to Barb Davis. Then they turned to look directly at her.

"Just a second, Charles," she said. She cupped the receiver in her hand and looked at the approaching officers. "May I help you?"

"Are you Teresa Miller?" the older of the two asked.

"Yes. What's wrong?"

"I'm afraid we have bad news," he said. "Your ex-husband, Darrell Cage, was found dead this morning, Miss Miller. He was identified by his driver's license, but they need you to make a positive identification."

"Darrell?" Tess felt a conspicuous lack of emotion at the news. In fact, she was more troubled by her lack of emotion than the fact of Darrell's death. "How did it happen?"

"He was stabbed," the younger one said, seeming to take great pleasure in his words. "Repeatedly."

"Oh, God."

Now she felt something, but it wasn't sadness for Darrell. That feeling might come later, but now, as she saw the blank accusation in the young cop's eyes, she felt a jolt of fear. She knew who the first suspect would be once they read the transcript of their divorce hearing. The list of people who disliked Darrell Cage was fairly substantial, but she knew full well that her name would be at the head of it.

"Could you come with us now?" the older policeman said.

It calmed Tess somewhat to see a look of disapproval in his eyes when he looked at his partner and to hear the softer tone of his voice. "Yes, I can. Oh, excuse me a second." Tess hurriedly spoke into the receiver again. "Charles? I'm sorry. Something has come up and I can't go to lunch after all."

She had tried to keep her tone neutral and businesslike, but he sensed something in it. "What's wrong?" he asked. "There's a problem, isn't there?"

"I have to go downtown to...ah...to identify my ex-husband's body," she said quickly. "I don't know what all that involves...."

"Oh, Tess, I'm so sorry," Charles said. "Look, I'll run downtown and meet you. Moral support and all that stuff."

"That's very kind—" she began.

"Not at all," he broke in. "Don't you worry about a thing. I'll meet you there."

He hung up before she had a chance to object again, and she could only replace the receiver and stand.

"Is there something wrong?" James Bentsen emerged from his office and approached them quickly. The look on his face said, "This interruption is costing us money." "Teresa, what's going on?"

"We've asked Miss Miller to come with us to identify a body, sir," the older officer said. "I don't think it will take too long, but then there may be other formalities."

"A body?" Mr. Bentsen looked at Tess as though she'd just been convicted of murder. "Well, I suppose that is serious," he told her, "but we do need the reports for this afternoon's meeting. Can you be back in time to do them?"

"I don't know," she said honestly. "I'll sure try."

"Well, I hope so," he sniffed.

"Should I follow you down?" she asked the policemen, ignoring her manager's idle fretting.

"You can ride with us," the officer said. "We'll bring you back when you're finished."

"Okay," she said. "Let's get it over with."

Tess left the office with the definite feeling that she wasn't going to get the report done in time for the meeting after all.

During her short but tense ride in the police car, Tess couldn't avoid the thought that she was being taken into custody rather than being driven to identify her husband's body. And why hadn't the police explained more? What exactly had happened? The attitude of the policemen and the way they tended to avoid making eye contact with her relayed the message that they thought her guilty. And if they thought it, how many others shared their feelings?

And now that they had her neatly caught, what was to say they wouldn't just keep her until they could build a case against her?

"YES, THAT'S DARRELL."

Having made her identification, she turned away

from the body quickly. Now she felt both shock and grief over his death. She wasn't reduced to tears, but at least the emotions were there. Tess had been afraid that she would continue to feel nothing even after seeing him dead in the cold white room.

"That's all we need from you, then," the coroner's assistant said. Los Palmas operated in conjunction with the Tampa coroner's office, and the man who handed her the clipboard for her signature was actually a local mortician. He was employed to do the preliminary work for the coroner when a death occurred.

"Do they have any idea who could have done this?" Tess asked him as she signed the form.

"Sorry, I can't tell you much about what happened," the man said. "I don't do the autopsies. It does look like he might have been stabbed with a steak knife, though."

"Why?"

"Well, I can't say for certain without further examination, but there's evidence that he was killed with a serrated blade. That, and the width of the wound, made it look like a steak knife."

"Gosh, I guess I'd better go home and count my silverware," Tess said, hoping to alleviate some of the tension with a bit of humor. When no one laughed, her own anxiety doubled. "Oh, Gabriel," she sighed, hoping the call would work once more. She really needed some support now, and Charles hadn't yet arrived to provide a more substantial shoulder to lean on.

"What's that?" the technician asked.

"Nothing," she said. "Just a curse of sorts."

"A curse is it? Well, I like that, I do." Gabriel's laughing voice came into her ear so quickly that she jumped. "Now don't you be leaping about like a startled deer or they'll think you're loony and throw away the key," he said.

"Is there something wrong?" the younger cop asked.

"No, nothing. Can I go now?"

"Be careful of that one, the younger of the two constables. He thinks you're guilty as hell. When he came to the house, he said he thought you'd gotten 'stiffed on alimony.'" Gabriel was close enough that she could feel his breath on the back of her neck as he spoke. "Be very careful with all of them, Tess, for they're none of them your friends and there are things you don't know."

She wanted to ask Gabriel what he meant by that, but the police were ushering her along the corridor too swiftly to find time for a whispered question. He had sounded suddenly serious, however, and it put her on her guard.

"We've got a couple of questions to ask you," the officer said. "It won't take long. Come along upstairs with us."

"Get ready to run, he should say," Gabriel said, "though I don't imagine that's the best plan for you at this moment. That young constable is a fine bastard, he is, but the gray-haired fellow is as much on your side as his kind is likely to get. He's the man to deal with, not that pup."

"What kind of questions are they?" Tess asked the older policeman, following Gabriel's advice as they walked to the elevator. "I don't know much about Darrell's whereabouts lately."

"We understand that." He used one courtly hand on her elbow to guide her into the elevator. "But we need to talk to everyone who knew him, and since you're here now, we might as well get it over with."

His partner followed them, turning to look curiously around before stepping into the car and allowing the doors to close. He looked confused as they rode upward and he kept rubbing his left ear.

"What's wrong with you?" the elder cop asked.

"Nothing," the young officer said quickly. "I just, well, I just felt something weird is all. It's nothing, I guess."

But when Tess turned to look at the man, she could see Gabriel Dyer standing at the officer's shoulder, happily flicking the tip of his finger at the man's ear. Then, with a wink, Gabriel disappeared from Tess's sight. She couldn't stop the grin that sprang to her lips then, and had to turn to hide it.

"That's it, Tess. Don't you get worried now. Keep a stout heart and I'll see you through it."

Her grin was short-lived, though. As the elevator doors opened, a scowling man in a brown suit was waiting for them.

"Oh, good, I caught you guys," he said. "Teresa Miller? I'm Detective Sergeant Wilkes, Los Palmas Police. I've got a warrant to search your premises." He handed her a folded paper as he spoke.

"What? I thought you just wanted to ask me some questions," Tess protested.

"We'll do that while we search," Wilkes told her. "I'll take her from here, men," he told the two officers.

Tess could do nothing but meekly accompany the man along the corridor, feeling as though each step was taking her irreversibly toward a jail cell. She felt absolutely certain that, in spite of her innocence and her lack of knowledge of the crime, she would be charged with Darrell's murder.

"Now's the time for running," Gabriel said in her ear. "But I'm afraid he'd shoot you down before you reached the door. The bloody fools would have you in fetters rather than look farther afield for the murderer. Constables haven't changed one bit. I only hope they don't ship convicts to Van Diemen's Land any longer."

No, but Tess rather wished they did, for she'd surely rather be in Australia right now than in Los Palmas, Florida.

Chapter Eight

"Tess, where are you off to now?" Charles Dumont shouted out to them as they crossed the parking lot to the detective's vehicle. Wilkes and Tess turned to wait for the banker to approach them. "I thought you had business here," he said when he reached them.

"And now she's business elsewhere," Sergeant Wilkes said to Charles. "Who are you?"

"Charles Dumont," said the banker with a touch of anger in his voice. "I'm a friend of this woman's. Who are you?"

"Detective Sergeant Wilkes," the policeman replied. "You say you're a friend? How so?"

"We have a personal relationship," Charles said. "Though I fail to see how it's any of your business."

"How long have you had this personal relationship?"

"What's that? Are you interrogating me in some manner?"

"Yes," the policeman said, "in some manner, I am. It's called conversation, a form of communication often involving simple questions. You say you're a friend of Teresa Miller's?"

"I like to think I am, yes," Charles said. "Although the degree of that friendship is up to the lady."

"And who is this self-important fellow you've got here now? I don't like the looks of him one bit," said Gabriel.

"He's a friend," Tess replied to Gabriel's question.

"Yes, I've been told that," Sergeant Wilkes said to her.

"He talks like a moneylender," added the pirate.

"Yes, he's a banker," she whispered.

"I'll let this guy explain himself if you don't mind," Wilkes said.

"No, I don't mind one bit."

Tess found herself laughing and was unable to stop herself for a moment. This was absurd. This policeman was looking for an excuse to arrest her, so Charles Dumont was arguing with the man and Gabriel was busy trying to annoy them by flicking at their ears. This whole thing was some kind of surreal comedy.

"What's so funny?" Wilkes asked.

"Nothing at all." Teresa restrained herself then and answered him soberly. "You are planning to arrest me, aren't you?"

"I don't know at the moment," the detective said. "All my warrant covers is a search of your home."

"I know, but you think I'm guilty, don't you? You plan to arrest me and then take a long lunch. Right?"

"Oh, now, don't get the man riled at you!" Gabriel cried out in her ear. "You're not fully informed about this thing!"

"No, actually, my kid's got an appointment with the orthodontist at one," Wilkes said. He seemed offended by her forthrightness. "So, I'm not planning on a long lunch."

"Oh, come now, you need not be evasive." Charles stepped into the conversation. "She asked a question and you should give her an answer."

"She's suspected of murdering her ex-husband, yes," Wilkes finally admitted. "Why would we search her home if she wasn't?" He turned his back on the banker, dismissing him from the conversation, and said to Tess, "You are his ex-wife, and you did make certain statements in open court that indicated a lack of friendliness on your part."

"Lack of friendliness?" Tess laughed again, unable to prevent her reaction to his tactful phrase. "Yes, I'd say that what I said about Darrell Cage would indicate a lack of friendliness. A big lack."

"Then you'd agree it's logical that we suspect you."

"Sure, for about five minutes," Tess said. "But I'm not in his will, for crying out loud! I've got nothing to gain by killing him! And I didn't hate him enough to do such a thing!"

"But you did hate him?"

"Tess, you'd better get a lawyer," Charles said warningly.

"Of course I hated him," Tess said. "But his business partners have more motive than I do. Are you checking on them?"

"Should we?"

"I don't know. It stands to reason that they'd have cause to murder him, though. After all, we are talking about Darrell Cage, aren't we? I never saw Darrell's books, but I'm an accountant, and there were telltale signs that he wasn't being entirely aboveboard in his financial dealings."

"And you think his partners stabbed him fourteen times with some kind of kitchen knife to get even?"

"Fourteen times?" Tess was taken aback by the information. Such savagery was unthinkable. "A woman would never do such a thing," she insisted.

"It's more common than you'd think in crimes of passion," Wilkes said.

"Oh, yes," Gabriel added. "I once saw a scullery maid slash a mate of mine over twenty strokes with a straight razor before we could put her down with a belaying pin."

"Quiet," Tess told the sailor.

"What?" Wilkes asked.

"Nothing," she said quickly. "I'm distraught."

"You'll be behind bars if you don't get a lawyer," Charles admonished.

"No, don't get tangled up with any lawyers!" Gabriel cried out. "They're worse than the constabulary and far more expensive!"

"Of course you can have a lawyer," Wilkes said. "That's your right under law. But I'm not charging you with anything now, only conducting a search. Or,

I should say, planning to conduct a search. If we ever get out of this parking lot, that is."

"Search away," she said. "I'm not stopping you."

"Into your home he'll be going? Lord, be careful, Tess, darlin'!" Gabriel said.

"I don't mind," Tess said. "I've got nothing to hide."

"He'll find something just the same. Don't taunt him."

"It's not a question of minding," Wilkes said. "I've got a warrant, so your opinion on the matter makes no difference."

"I'll call a lawyer," Charles said, his gaze shifting between Tess and the policeman with shrewd appraisal.

"No, don't bother," Tess said. "I can't afford one anyway."

"Why does this man want to pay your lawyer for you anyway?"

"Come on, I've got men waiting at your house," Wilkes said.

"Busily planting evidence all the while, I'll wager," Gabriel said. "You'd better get home before they can do more damage."

"I'm coming along," Charles said.

"No, you are not," Wilkes said. Taking Tess by the arm, he began walking to his car once more. "You are going to stay well away from this investigation, or I'll have you thrown in the can for obstructing justice. Got that?"

"Certainly," Charles said. "But I'm not going to stand idly by and watch an innocent woman railroaded into jail."

"No, I don't suppose you would." Wilkes ushered Tess into the passenger seat of his vehicle and then hurried around to open his door. "Call your lawyer or whatever else you want to do. Just stay out of my way until I want to borrow money," he told the banker. "Goodbye, Mr. Dumont."

They pulled out of the parking spot with a lurch and then moved to join the midmorning traffic.

"Have you known Dumont long?" Wilkes asked as he drove.

"No," Tess said, morosely watching an airplane approaching the Tampa airport. Dark clouds were building up overhead as they drove. She wondered what cares and worries the airplane passengers brought with them. Surely, no one else had troubles as bad as hers.

"He acts as if he's known you a long time."

"He hasn't."

"The guy's a jerk."

"He does like to sound important," she admitted.

As she said it, she realized for the first time that it was true. He wasn't the type of person who spoke constantly of his many duties and responsibilities, but he dismissed his responsibilities in an offhand manner that made it seem he was extremely important. It was as if he were so capable that he could discount his own importance. It was an interesting way of drawing attention to himself while appearing to be pushing it away.

Of course, he'd been calling attention to himself quite vehemently today. She supposed it was a misguided attempt to draw official ire away from her by being obnoxious. It hadn't worked, though. No, Detective Sergeant Wilkes wasn't the type to be distracted.

"So this personal relationship he spoke of isn't all he likes to imply?" the officer said.

"No. We went out Sunday night," Tess said. Then she scowled, regarding the policeman behind the wheel stonily. "I've known him about a day and a half, Sergeant. Does that cover the topic fully?"

"I suppose so," he said, impervious to the anger in her voice. "I've noticed that when people wade in offering to call lawyers before there's any need of them, it's sometimes a sign they suspect the person is guilty."

"Why do you think that?"

"Because honest people usually don't think about lawyers until we advise them to call one."

"I haven't asked to call a lawyer," she remarked.

"No, you haven't," he said, nodding his head. "So why does this friend of yours think you need one?"

"How should I know?"

"Because he's a guilty sod himself is why," Gabriel said suddenly in Tess's ear.

"What?"

"I didn't say anything," Wilkes said as he turned onto her street.

"Sorry," Tess said.

"He's a banker, is he not?" Gabriel persisted. "Think of all those he's turned out into the street, the houses and businesses he's foreclosed on. He's a guilty sod, all right."

Tess smiled wryly. Her ghostly friend certainly had his own point of view on the matter.

They pulled into her driveway behind a black-and-white police cruiser. Two officers stood waiting beside it. Wilkes stopped and got out quickly, saying, "Okay, let's do it. And keep it neat."

"Gabriel," Tess whispered quickly before she got out of the car, "if you're going to follow me around like this, I'd really prefer that you don't talk to me. You're going to have everyone thinking I'm crazy before this is over."

"Fine, but you mind yourself with these fellows," he advised.

"I will," she promised. Then she got out of the car and ran to unlock her door for the officers.

DETECTIVE SERGEANT Wilkes and the two uniformed officers conducted a thorough search of Tess's house. The warrant only gave them the power to look for a murder weapon or "evidence of intention to commit murder" hidden on her property "real or rental."

With this in mind, they confiscated most of her sharp knives, leaving her with a dull paring knife and an even duller butcher knife.

They overturned the cushions of her chairs and couches, the mattress on her bed and checked the entire contents of every closet in her house. They sorted through every drawer, took down the stacked items on every shelf and peered beneath any loose carpeting and throw rugs.

It was a very thorough search indeed. But as far as Tess could tell, it yielded nothing.

"Your home was broken into, and you were nearly burglarized this past night, and these ruffians have you in their sights when they should be trying to uncover the identity of that criminal," Gabriel said harshly. He'd remained quiet through most of the search, but the sight of the men looking through her dresser drawers was too much for him.

"Shhh," Tess said.

"Shush as you will, but it's still a shame."

Yes, it was a shame, but they didn't know about the break-in. Everything had happened with such shocking speed that she hadn't even thought to tell them about the intruder. Besides, only Gabriel had seen the man. Now she felt certain that it was too late to bring up the incident. Sergeant Wilkes would assume she was mentioning it only to provide an explanation for anything they might find. He'd be prompted to search even harder.

"When did your divorce from Darrell Cage become final?"

Detective Sergeant Wilkes sat on a chair opposite her at the kitchen table and opened his notebook.

"Three months ago."

"Did you have many occasions to see him since then?"

"More than I wanted," Tess said. "I mean, well, no, I guess that's what I meant."

It annoyed her that her every word might make her seem suspect to these men. She wasn't used to watching her words so closely.

"Did he bother you?"

"He didn't seem to think divorce was a very good idea."

"Why not?"

"Probably because one of his lady friends might have started talking about marriage if he didn't already have a wife at home," she said bitterly.

"Played the field, did he?" Wilkes was writing in his notebook as he spoke. "More than one affair?"

"Probably. I don't know of more than one."

"Was he ever abusive?"

"He was drunk a lot," she said. "The abuse went with that."

"He hit you?"

"Twice," she admitted.

"It's good the rogue is dead," Gabriel said quietly from somewhere behind Tess.

"How long were you married?"

"Five years. A little more," she said. It was hard to believe they lasted that long, but then Tess had believed in marriage, hoped she could make things work.

"He was three years older than you?" Wilkes pressed on. Her answers were just raw data to him, facts to be fed into his investigation.

"Yes. I was still in college when I met him."

A fat raindrop hit the kitchen window as they spoke, then another and another. It would be pouring soon, and that seemed appropriate.

"The real-estate business was his old man's, right?"

"Yes. Darrell wouldn't have had the patience to build it up himself," she said. "He liked things easy."

"You work as an accountant, you said. Have you been working since college? Ever do any accounting for him?"

"No. Darrell didn't want me to work, and we didn't need the extra money."

"You just did as he said?" Wilkes asked, one eyebrow raised. "Excuse me, but you don't strike me as that type of woman."

"Sergeant Wilkes, would you work if you didn't have to?"

The man paused a second, then a smile touched his lips briefly. "No," he admitted, "I'd go fishing."

"Well, I guess I went fishing," she said.

"But you're working now."

"Yes, I am definitely working now."

"Your husband was here last night?"

"He wasn't my husband," she corrected him. "Yes, he was here. He tried to get rough with me, but I managed to throw him out."

"You threw him out? What are you, about five foot five? A hundred and ten or so?"

"Five-six, and my weight is none of your business."

"Okay, but you threw him out of your house?"

"Did a fine job of throwing, too," Gabriel whispered.

"He was more than a little bit drunk."

"Must have been," Wilkes commented. He wrote something down.

"You don't think I just threw him out," she said. "I'll bet that you think I stabbed him to death instead."

"Not in this house, you didn't."

"So why are you even searching the place?"

"His car was parked two houses down the block from here," Wilkes said. "It looks like he went off with someone, figuring to come back for it."

"And you figure that we went for a moonlight drive together—maybe in my car, right?" Tess said, suddenly quite angry. "You people are insane. What did I do? Stab him to death with a steak knife? Is that what I did? But why would he go anywhere in my rusted old heap when his fabulous car was parked outside? How could I talk him into that?"

"I don't know," Wilkes said. "We've got both cars in the police garage now to check them out."

"My car? You even hauled my car in? Well, I guess I should be glad it's not sitting out in the rain with the windows open. Thank you for that."

"Miss Miller," Wilkes said sourly, "I'm not terribly interested in what you think of how I do my job. A man was killed, and you're a very good suspect. That's all I know at this time."

"And it's all you care to know, too."

"No, I'd like to know who killed Darrell Cage. If it's not you, then I want to know who. That's all."

"And when you do catch his killer, will I get a nice apology for all the trouble you've put me through?"

"No, you won't. You are a suspect in a murder investigation. That's all there is to it."

"Listen!" she snapped. "I was unemployed for over eight months while I was getting my divorce! I drive a worn-out old car because I had to sell my new car to pay rent. But I didn't go back to Darrell, and I didn't kill him in all that time. Why on earth would I kill him now that I've got a job and I'm due for a raise in just over two weeks? My rent is paid, there's food in the fridge, and I'm almost caught up on my utilities. And yet I choose *now* to kill that weasel? I'd be rich if I had killed him when we were still married, so why would I wait until I wouldn't gain anything by it?"

"I didn't say you planned to kill him," Wilkes said calmly. "It just happened."

"I'm as good as locked away for life as far as you're concerned, aren't I? Maybe I should have let Charles get me that lawyer."

"I'll tell you when you need a lawyer."

"Sarge?" One of the officers came into the kitchen then. "We're finished in here. There's nothing else."

"Okay." Wilkes stood, looking out the window at the rain that fell steadily now. "Whose garage is that?"

"My landlord's," Tess told him.

"Take a look in there," he told the officer. "The side door might be open."

The officer looked sourly at the garage through the rain. "Right," he said. Then he opened the kitchen door and sprinted across the lawn to the garage, where the side door was, indeed, open.

"Oh, God Almighty!" Gabriel exclaimed. "We were so close to being shut of them! Don't let them in the yard, lass! Don't on your life let them search the yard."

"Don't call me lass," Tess whispered, though some intangible feeling told her that her invisible friend had left the room. She rubbed her eyes, feeling worn-out.

"I didn't say anything," Wilkes said. He laid a sheet of paper on the table before her and held his pen out. "Sign this," he told her.

"What is it?"

"It's a form stating that we didn't break anything in our search. Insurance business," he said.

"I'd better check...no, why bother?" she said. "I'll take your word for it."

Taking the pen, she signed the document and pushed it back across to him.

"You're left-handed," he remarked.

"Yes, I'm left-handed. Is that a crime, too?"

"No." He folded the paper and slipped it into the inner pocket of his suit jacket.

"Sergeant!" A call from outside brought their attention to the yard. The uniformed officer was running back to the house from the garage, a plastic bag swinging loosely in one hand. "Sarge, I found it!" he exclaimed as he burst into the kitchen.

"What is it?" Wilkes asked, approaching the officer and taking the clear plastic bag from him. Then he smiled, turned to Tess and dropped the bag onto her kitchen table.

Inside the sealed Ziploc bag lay a steak knife similar to the odd assortment of knives they'd already taken from her kitchen. This knife, however, was unmistakably coated with blood!

"Miss Teresa Miller," Detective Sergeant Wilkes said, "you are under arrest for the murder of Darrell Cage. Now you need a lawyer. And you'd better keep quiet until you get one."

The advice wasn't necessary, in any case, for Tess couldn't think of a thing to say. All she could do was stare at the knife on the table—the knife which, in all probability, had been used to kill Darrell Cage.

Chapter Nine

"You will have to go through booking, of course, but their evidence is rather flimsy so I don't expect you to spend the night."

Walter Chambers, the lawyer Charles had found for her defense was a stout fellow with thinning blond hair and tinted glasses. He looked as though he'd be more at home chasing ambulances for whiplash claims than handling a murder defense, but, in his favor, he didn't promise any miracles and didn't smile overly much as some lawyers she'd known had done. The attorney she'd used for her divorce, for instance.

"Is that knife all they've got?" she asked hopefully. "No witnesses?"

"Should there be witnesses?" he asked straightforwardly.

Tess shook her head emphatically. "No, of course not."

"Listen, I know all that stuff they say on TV about never asking a client if they're guilty," Chambers said. "It's a fine, optimistic way to go about life to think everyone innocent—especially your own clients. But this is a different matter. Spousal abuse is a big deal these days. So, Teresa, if you are guilty of killing the creep, then please tell me now. If you don't—"

"Mr. Chambers, I—"

"No, wait, don't cut me off while I'm at the point in my speech where I look like I don't believe in you. Let me redeem myself by saying that on the face of it you look innocent to me. I think the knife was a plant. But I've been wrong before, and I'd rather start out knowing everything than have surprises pop up in the end. So, did you do it?"

"No," Tess said flatly. "I wanted to, though."

"Honest. I like that." He did smile then, and he removed his glasses to rub his eyes while working a kink out of his neck. "You won't believe how people can suddenly find deep wells of respect for guys they hated in life, especially if they're accused of killing them. Frankly, it looks false to judges and juries."

"We're raised not to speak ill of the dead," Tess offered.

The attorney sighed. "So, how many times did he hit you?" he asked gently.

"Twice," she said. "Once when he was roaring drunk after a big land deal fell through. The second time was when I told him I'd hired a lawyer to get a divorce."

"It wasn't habitual?"

"No, Darrell was a braggart and a creep, but not really a physical person."

"What about the knife? Did it look like one of yours?"

"It could be," she admitted. "I rented the place furnished, and that included everything. The flat-ware is a rather eclectic mix of stuff, and I'd say there were at least three different sets of steak knives mixed together in the drawer."

"All right, then, the knife bears only a superficial resemblance to what you've got." He made a note on his pad. "They found it in the garage. Your car wasn't in the garage at the time?"

"No, the police impounded it. Besides, I don't rent the garage."

"What?" He stopped, pen poised over the paper. "You don't have use of that garage?"

"No, I only rented the house. My landlord uses the garage for storage."

For a moment, he just stared at her as a tentative smile slowly crept onto his lips.

"And you have no use of the garage at all?" he asked. "No key? Nothing of yours is stored in there?"

"No, of course not."

"That's it!" He slapped his palm down on his legal pad and stood, grinning. "You're clear, Teresa, and they can throw that knife in the trash!"

"Why? What are you talking about?"

"This is great!" he exclaimed, slapping the table again in happiness. "Look, the house you live in is your property because you've paid for the right to call it such. The search warrant covered your property, real or rental, and only your property! See? That knife wasn't on your property! That means that it was illegally obtained during a search and, as evidence, it just doesn't exist! It's no good, and will never be any good, in court!''

"Really?"

"Exactly. It was a sloppy search, and you'll be out of here in little more than an hour." He shuffled his papers together and folded his pad to leave. "They'll probably still finish the booking, but that's as far as it'll go. Don't you worry."

"But if they messed up their search, why should they book me at all?"

"I'll have a judge get you out of here," he said, ignoring her rhetorical question. "The cops aren't going to admit anything about falsely obtaining their evidence unless I force them to do it. Don't worry, I'll have you out in ninety minutes, max!"

"Okay, I'll tough it out," she promised. "It seems a bit too good to be true, though."

"It's true," he assured her. He buzzed for the guard to let him out of the interrogation room. "Unless you know something about this that you aren't telling me, that's all there is to it."

"I don't know anything else," she said.

"Okay, then. They've got your prints, so they'll take you down to the cells now. I've got to find a judge and get my paperwork in order before they all go home for the night. 'Bye now," he said as the door beside him opened. "Ninety minutes, max."

"Goodbye."

With her lawyer gone, Tess found herself alone. The day's events were still so fresh and so unbelievable that she just sat in shock for a minute until a voice in her ear reminded her that she wasn't really alone at all.

"So, am I to take it that they're forced to ignore that knife just because it was found on another man's property?" Gabriel sounded skeptical. "A resourceful criminal would surely have known that fact and acted accordingly."

"But a resourceful police department would have thought about it before looking in that garage."

"True."

"Gabriel, could you please let me see you if you're going to be talking to me?" Tess asked him. "You're making me crazy talking out of nowhere like that."

"That wasn't my desire." He materialized across the table seated in the chair her lawyer had vacated. Or, more correctly, he was kneeling in front of the chair so that it looked as though he was seated. "But then I think it would take far more than a spirit voice to make you crazy, Tess Miller."

"Why do you think that?" She rubbed her forehead, watching the man across from her grow from a faint image to that of a solid, real human being. "I feel like a wimp."

"Wimp? Weakling, I suppose," he mused. "No, you're hardly that." His smile seemed to soften the light in the room, making her feel safer. "You put that officer of the law in his place, you did, and you haven't buckled under the pressure of any of this. You're a strong woman, Tess Miller, a fine woman."

"Thank you," she said. "I just hope I'm a free woman soon."

"You will be," he said.

The door of the interrogation room opened and a policewoman entered. "Come on," she said, her hands and forearms sliding through the smiling pirate's chest. She pulled her hands back abruptly, frowning. "Let's get you settled in," she said with less certainty.

"I suppose you'll be needing money to pay that lawyer, then," Gabriel said. "As sure as it rains, a lawyer wants his money. You don't want that banker fellow paying the freight."

"No," Tess said quietly.

"You're not going to sit here all night," the officer said tightly. "Come on."

"I wasn't—oh, never mind." Tess stood and walked to the door with her.

"You get out of here," Gabriel said, "and we'll go about rounding up some money for your legal defense. Unless, of course, a pirate's booty has no value these days."

Tess merely nodded, hoping he would take that as confirmation of the value of his contribution. She followed the woman down the hall and through a steel door into a room containing a table and several lockers.

"Okay, remove your clothing," the policewoman said, sliding a manila envelope across the table. "Put your valuables into this envelope."

"What?"

"Strip," the woman commanded. "We've got to conduct a search, and then you'll wear the prison jumpsuit. Hurry up and it'll be over within a minute."

"But my lawyer will be back—"

"Sure, sure, but you've still got to be searched."

Resigned, Tess slipped out of her shoes and began unbuttoning her blouse. Then she stopped, saying, "Get out of here, Gabriel. Okay?"

"What?" the woman asked.

"I'm gone," said Gabriel, and Tess was privy to the strange sight of the man backing out through a solid wall. As he disappeared, he said, "Don't you let them rile you, lass. You're a singular woman, and I've all the faith in the world that you're up to this challenge. If I were a man instead of a foolish spirit, I'd find ways to back up my words and let you know the truth of them. Goodbye for now, lass."

And, at that moment, hearing the heartfelt tone of his words, Tess didn't mind being called lass at all.

"WE'VE GOT TO KEEP the cops focused on the wife," Carl Downey said. "As long as they're busy looking for ways to pin it on her, they won't try pinning it on us."

Carl was sitting in his office at Downey Construction with Jay Sturgis, his "assistant," seated across the broad desk from him. Carl was in his mid-sixties, balding, but still as lean as he had been when he was a middleweight prizefighter years earlier. Stout and short, Jay was in his late thirties with dark hair and eyes.

"The last I heard was that they found a knife," Jay said. "Her lawyer went to see a judge about springing her, but I don't see how he can fight that evidence."

"Walter Chambers is her lawyer," Carl said, smiling smugly. "No way he'll get her off. He's just a two-bit crook. It would be nice if she actually did kill the guy. *Someone* had to do it."

"Do you think she did, Carl?"

"No, but it's good that the cops think she did."

"We've got the title with her signature," Jay reminded him. "We can forge her name on the other paperwork."

"No, I don't want anything to go wrong. There's too much money tied up in this to blow it all by forging the woman's signature." Carl sighed, looking out the window at the gray sky. "I think we'll just have to cut our losses and buy the land from her. If anything looks untoward, we won't be suspected."

"We already bought the land once."

"I know," Carl said ruefully. "But it's the price we'll have to pay for doing business with a shifty fool like Cage. Draw up some purchase papers so we can get it over and done with. Even a conviction won't help. That'll keep them from digging into his business affairs too deeply, but it won't help this deal. We want to break ground in a month—not after years in court."

"Okay, I'll get right on it."

Carl Downey continued looking out the window as the other man left the room. Everything had been going so well until Cage's wife decided to divorce him. Dealing with the now-deceased Realtor had been less than satisfactory since then. All because of that woman. Maybe she did kill him. Maybe not. If she didn't, he'd better keep an eye out for who did. There was a lot of money involved after all.

THE WHEELS OF JUSTICE turn at their own pace, and the wheels turned slowly enough that Tess suffered the indignity of a jailhouse meal before her lawyer returned with an order for her release.

"I'm horribly sorry for the delay," Chambers said. "The judge was backlogged, and the cops put a lot of effort into covering their rears. Sergeant Wilkes has a lieutenant's exam coming up, and he's very anxious about that."

He met her outside the cell block after she'd changed clothing.

"At least I'm out," Tess said. "Now what?"

She had decided that she couldn't tell Walter Chambers about the intruder, either. As an officer of the court, he was obligated to tell the police. Maybe the cops would suspect both her and Chambers of trying to create a nonexistent housebreaker to pin the crime on.

"They'll try to make their case in some other way," he said. "Don't be too surprised if you see some ill-concealed police officers following you from time to time. Darrell Cage was worth millions. This case is a big deal for them, and now that they've officially pegged you as a suspect, they'll hold on to you like a dog with a bone."

"Gee, thanks, you've made me feel much better," she said. "Where do I get my belongings?"

"At the front desk."

They walked to the booking desk, where the envelope containing her personal effects was unceremoniously given to her and she was told not to leave town. When she stepped out of the police station into a light drizzle, Tess felt so good that the sky might have been bright and cloudless.

"Now what do I do?" she asked Chambers.

"We get your car out of the impound and then you go about your life as best you can."

"And that's it? Where does the police investigation go from here?"

"If we're lucky, and I mean damn lucky, they'll get a lead away from you and eventually catch the killer," he said seriously. "If we're unlucky, they'll concentrate on proving that you did it and never leave you alone. Remember, as far as the cops are concerned, you got out of this on a technicality."

"So they still believe I'm guilty."

"Yes, they believe you're guilty."

"They will leave me alone, won't they? I mean, I can go on with my life more or less normally?"

"Yes, more or less," he said as they walked down the steps and around the corner to the parking lot and its fenced-in section reserved for impounded vehicles. "They have probable cause to keep you under surveillance if they want to, but not to harass you or impede you in any way. If you have any trouble with them, call me and I'll slap an injunction on them."

"Thank you," she said. "It's good to know I've got someone on my side in all this mess."

There was no one visible in the lot, so Walter pressed the buzzer on the door to the garage.

"You've got Charles Dumont in your corner, too," he said.

"Yes, I guess I do. Say, about your fee . . ." she began.

"Mr. Dumont will cover that."

"No, he won't, either," Tess said quickly. "He's a nice guy and all that, but I'd rather not owe him for my defense. Okay? I'll pay you myself."

"Fine," Chambers said. "I'll just bill you by the hour and send it to you when we're all done."

"Good. I'm making arrangements to get the cash now. Would a week be too long to get the money?"

"I hate to dampen your mood," he said, smiling. "But I'm going to be your lawyer for much longer than a week. Unless they come up with a killer in record time, you won't have to worry about paying your bill till sometime around Christmas."

"That long? They won't be watching me all that time, will they?"

"No, they don't have the manpower, but they'll sure keep it open."

He pushed the buzzer again. This time, an officer opened the door. "Yes?" the uniformed man asked.

"Walter Chambers," the lawyer said. "We've come for Teresa Miller's car. Here's the paperwork."

The officer took the papers from the lawyer suspiciously and looked them over. Apparently satisfied with the vehicle release form, he nodded and said, "Just a minute." A moment later, he emerged from a door on the other side of the chain-link fence and unlocked the gate. "Back row," he said brusquely, handing her the car keys.

As Tess accepted them, she felt the first hint of what it would be like to be under the constant suspicion of the police department, for the man stared at her with open contempt, branding her a murderer with his eyes.

"Happy motoring," the officer said.

"You'll have to learn to ignore them," Chambers advised as they walked to the car, which was parked between a dented Chevy and a Cadillac. "They aren't going to go out of their way to make it easy on you."

"I can tell," Tess said. "Well, thank you for everything."

"It was a pleasure," he said. "I'll call you if there are any further developments, and I want you to call me if the police give you any trouble at all. Just don't leave town. Don't even appear to be leaving town."

"I won't," she promised, unlocking her car door. "Oh, by the way, nobody ever said exactly where they found the body."

"On the beach near Bernie's Lounge," he said. "Does that mean anything to you?"

"No," she replied a bit doubtfully. It did seem odd the killer wouldn't have chosen a more secluded spot than that. Unless, of course, he wanted the body to be found as quickly as possible. "Well, thank you again."

Her lawyer acknowledged her thanks with a thumbs-up and then turned and walked away.

"Well, then, you're out, are you?" Gabriel appeared in the back seat, startling her briefly.

Tess grinned, shaking her head. "We're going to have to work on your manners," she chided. "Popping in and out just won't do. Where have you been?" she asked as she drove out of the impound lot and headed north toward home. "I missed you."

"You did?" He sounded surprised and pleased, and Tess looked into her rearview mirror to see a broad smile lighting his features. "I didn't feel that I should be staying as it was a women's jail and all. I could admit, however, that I missed you, as well. I missed you a great deal."

"There were only two cells for women," she said. "And I was the only woman there."

"Well, I put my time to good use," he said. "I've done a bit of reconnoitering, and I believe I can find my booty just off the beach a bit."

"You mean the bag of money you threw overboard?"

"Yes, though I don't expect the bag has survived. Gold, it held, and gems. Perhaps that lawyer fellow could help you convert old booty into ready cash."

"I imagine he can," Tess said. "I don't know much about salvage laws."

"I know less, that's certain," Gabriel said. He leaned forward, resting one muscular forearm on the seat beside her while he watched her drive. "So what manner of transportation is this?"

"An automobile," she replied, glad to have something to talk about rather than the murder. "We also call them cars. They run on gasoline."

"And you all ride around by yourselves in them just as a person might ride a horse, even though you've got the space of a carriage inside?"

"Yes, exactly."

"Don't you get lonely riding by yourself all the time?"

"No, not usually. It's very wasteful, though."

"Aye, that it is. But you do it well," he commented. "I've felt nary a bump."

"I can teach you how to drive if you'd like."

"I would," he said. "From what I've seen, a person who cannot manipulate one of these vehicles is as good as cast adrift in the world."

"Tomorrow after work, I'll show you how," she promised. "If you're still here, that is."

"Where else should I be?"

"I don't know," Tess answered, frowning. "I'm afraid you'll be snatched away just as quickly as you came. I wouldn't like that."

"Nor would I. Tess Miller, I find you to be a wonderful woman, and I'd like nothing better than to remain with you. It's very strange that after all those years of wishing I'd be gone somehow, I find myself wishing not to go."

"That's very kind of you to say."

"'Tis the truth. I feel as if I've known you a long time, Tess Miller. I know that I was meant to be here with you."

Though she couldn't find the right words to express her own emotions, she knew her feelings for him were the same. She felt comfortable with Gabriel, as though his presence was a woolly blanket she could snuggle under to keep the cold world at bay. She felt—well, she felt loved when she was with him. There was no other word than that.

"Have you given any more thought to why you're here at all?" Tess asked. "For that matter, do you know of any way you might cross over completely? You know, become totally alive again?"

"I've thought about that quite extensively," he said. "I would give a king's ransom to feel the sand beneath my feet and taste a tankard of ale once more. I'd gladly die another time if I had but an hour to touch..." He let his words trail off, then looked out at the buildings.

"We'll have to work on that," Tess said, wishing he had finished what he'd begun to say. She could see in her rearview mirror, however, that he was frowning. "What's wrong?"

"Oh, I am that transparent, am I, that you can tell my mood so easily?" He smiled then, but it was forced. "It's true enough that something is eating at me, but I'd rather talk about it in the safety of your home rather than here on the open roadway."

"Safety? Gabriel, I am safe," she said. "Is there something you don't want to tell me?"

"Oh, I want to and will," he said quickly.

"Then tell me now," she insisted, shifting her gaze between the evening traffic and the man's face in her mirror.

"I've lied to you, Tess, and that bothers me. It was a sin of omission to be sure, and with good intent, but I'm still not at ease with it. This morning, when you left the house, everything went as we planned. I lost my hunger right enough and was able to leave the house, as well. I thought it necessary to have a look at that small yard behind your house."

"Yes?" His tone warned her to be ready for bad news, but she couldn't think of what it could possibly be.

He touched her shoulder, his broad hand massaging her gently. "There was blood in the yard," he said. "A great quantity of blood. You see, lass, I would bet that your husband was, indeed, killed on your premises last night. If the constables had taken any more time in the yard, they'd have seen where the body was dragged away."

"Oh, God," she exclaimed, "that's why you said not to let them into the yard."

"Yes, that's it. I thank God for the rain, but it wasn't quite soon enough."

"Do you think that sound I heard last night was when it happened? Gabriel, this is horrible! I should have let you check it out right then."

Tess had to concentrate on her driving with extra care, for her heart was suddenly beating so hard that it seemed to shake the car.

"No, then you would have been at the mercy of the killer caught in the act," he said. "I couldn't have helped you, Tess."

"Why didn't you tell me before? Gabriel, I should have known! Just because I'm a woman, that doesn't mean I need protection from the truth!"

"That had nothing at all to do with it, lass," he insisted. "There just wasn't the time. But also I didn't want you to have to lie to them when they asked their questions. As it is, you're innocent on all counts."

"Then the man at my door..."

"Was probably on his way to do away with you," Gabriel finished for her. "It was only the best of luck that allowed me to be there to stop him."

"Oh, dear God," she sighed.

"Don't you worry now, because forewarned is forearmed. No one will harm you while I'm about."

But Tess knew that his assurance wouldn't stop her worrying and her mind was swirling in a fog of anxiety and confusion as she continued driving home. Why would anyone want to kill either her or Darrell? There was no sense to it, but it seemed clear that someone was planning to do exactly that.

Every car that passed on the street suddenly seemed suspicious to Tess. Every person who glanced her way as she drove seemed to have a killer's eyes. There was no way of knowing who or why—she only knew that someone wanted to kill her!

Her only defense was her knowledge and a man whose protection amounted to little more than a whisper in her ear!

Chapter Ten

They were driving into the outskirts of town, crossing through a retail area near her neighborhood, when a large K mart sign in the distance gave her an idea.

"I know what we'll do now. I don't suppose you know your measurements, do you?"

"No, I'm no tailor."

"Well, then, I'll guess. The least I can do is to get you something to wear so you don't have to squeeze into my ratty old sweatpants anymore."

An hour later, she parked the car in front of her house and hurried up the steps with several bags of masculine apparel in her arms. It had felt good to have something to do that could take her mind off the murder and her ordeal with the police. And it felt good to be doing something for a man who appreciated her efforts.

Gabriel was well pleased with the clothing and eager to dress himself in a manner that would please Tess. He enjoyed the pleasure she took in picking out a wardrobe for him. In fact, he found that he enjoyed just about anything she enjoyed simply because of the pleasure she found in it.

Outfitting the pirate proved to be more of a task than merely buying clothing and putting it on him. Just as with the apple and her rented furniture, Gabriel was unable to touch any of what she bought, and they were at a loss until Tess realized that she would have to wear the clothes first. So, Tess went about straightening up the house wearing a man's T-shirt and jeans that dragged loosely on the floor when she walked. She was even wearing the white cotton briefs beneath the trousers, while Gabriel continued wearing her black sweats.

The maneuver was successful, however, and he was soon dressed and seated on a kitchen chair.

"You are the connection I have to this earth, that much is certain," Gabriel said, watching her eat. "I'm here for you, Tess Miller. And you for me."

"Why?" she asked.

"Why not?" he replied. "I can touch only what you have touched. And I can touch you." He moved his hand up, the bare forearm passing through the table where they sat, and placed his hand on her cheek. "You're warm," he said. "The only warmth I can feel is your warmth. Your skin has the texture of the finest silk, and that much I can feel. I feel no other warmth, and nothing else has much texture. But you feel complete beneath my hand. I feel a connection to you, Teresa. Don't you feel at least a little of the same?"

"Yes," she admitted. "I just don't know why."

"You ask why far too often," he said. "A person can grow old waiting to find out the why of things."

"I thought you were an hallucination at first," she said. "I was afraid I was losing my mind. Now I don't know what to think, though I'll admit I like the idea of our connection. If you were a real man—I mean, a living man—I'd gladly accept it at face value. But it seems forced this way. I mean, you don't really have any choice, do you? I'm your one and only connection to the world."

With his hand still firmly on her cheek, Tess felt herself wishing she could just forget logic and go along with the events taking place without looking for reasons. What had happened to her that day proved how insecure and unpredictable life was, but she still couldn't help asking questions.

"I have a choice," he said, bringing his other hand up to caress her cheek. "I made it years ago, you see, and I think you are very much the same person I chose back then. Camille was much like you. Neither of you would accept a gift without seeing the bill of sale, so to speak. Yet you share her capacity to enjoy life. Some people, you know, can never find it in themselves to have a bit of fun. Others have nothing but. You and my dear wife fall between the two. You have sense enough to come in out of a storm, but spirit enough to enjoy it, as well."

"What do you mean?"

"I mean that if I were to travel the world over, I'd not find anyone more suited to my own temperament than yourself. I mean that I'm glad to be here with you and that I will stay willingly to do what I can to help you and comfort you for as long as the Fates allow me to do so."

"Gabriel, I—"

The telephone rang, cutting off Tess's ill-formed thoughts. She rose from the table to answer the phone. She'd hardly said hello before a breathless voice broke in.

"Tess! My God! How are you?" It was Betty Crown, barely able to contain her excitement. "I saw it on the TV news of all places! They arrested you? Are they insane?"

"I was on the news?" Tess groaned.

"You certainly were! Hey, babe, you don't knock off the hottest young real-estate tycoon in town and not get some press! And they said you were released, too. Can they do that? It's a murder charge, isn't it?"

"Well, I didn't do it," Tess said.

"So they're dropping the charges?"

"Not exactly, but they don't have enough evidence to hold me."

"What are you supposed to do now?"

"My lawyer says to try going on with my life as usual and hope they find someone else to pin it all on."

As she spoke to her friend, Tess watched Gabriel stand and walk to the living room. She wished she could tell Betty about him, but she wasn't eager to open herself up to the teasing she'd get. Who would believe she was on a first-name basis with a ghost?

"What happened at work this afternoon?" she asked. "I imagine Bentsen was a bit annoyed."

"More than a bit," Betty said. "And I don't suppose the evening news helped his disposition any. It could be a frosty morning. Are you coming in?"

"I don't have much choice, Betty. It's my job."

"Well, it'll be interesting, anyway."

"All I need is another interesting day. I'd better get off the phone now and go to bed," Tess told her friend. "I'm exhausted."

"You must be beat. Try to get a good night's rest. See you tomorrow, hon."

"'Bye."

Tess hung up the phone, feeling as though a special moment between her and Gabriel had been lost. Whatever it was they had been in the mood to say to each other wasn't going to be said now. But she hoped there would soon be another time.

"What did the man look like?" she asked Gabriel when she joined him in the living room.

"The moonlight was behind him, so my vision of the fellow was obscured. Fair-haired, I think. Yes, I can say that much."

"How tall was... Oh, this is foolish," she said. "Even if you could describe him perfectly, I'm sure I wouldn't know who he is, and we could never find him anyway."

"We shall have to, though, won't we?"

"Why would anyone want to kill both Darrell and me?"

"What about the man's business? I understand that the cad was well-off. He must have ruffled a few feathers in order to gain his wealth."

"He inherited it," she said absently. "Wait, you know he didn't exactly play by the rules. He signed several pieces of property over to me while we were married. Later, as I began to doubt his character, I started to assume that was to keep his name off the deeds.''

"To conceal ownership when it came to selling it again, no doubt," Gabriel said. "He was earning his money twice in one way or another. Maybe there's someone out there who wasn't too happy with that."

"That's possible," she admitted. "And since I was the fool who signed the papers, I might well be singled out for that reason."

"Yes, lass, it's a possibility." Gabriel seemed less certain now, though. "Your husband was a jealous type, wasn't he?"

"Oh, yes."

"Well, then, maybe he was killed by accident."

"What?"

"I'm thinking now that he was skulking about in your yard because he thought you had a man in here with you."

"That's what I thought, too. Oh, no, I see what you mean." Tess stood and walked to the kitchen window and looked out over the dark yard. Momentarily cold, she shivered, thinking of the crime that had been committed there last night. "How would anyone trying to kill Darrell know he was in my yard?" she questioned, turning back toward Gabriel. "Even if someone were following him, why kill him here and drag him away?"

"If the culprit was after the both of you, he'd surely have done you both in and let it go at that."

"Nobody was trying to kill Darrell. No, I'm sure he was only sneaking through the yard trying to keep an eye on me! Yes, he was just in the wrong place at the wrong time!''

''I could accept that,'' Gabriel said. ''But that means, you realize, that the killer is after you alone.''

''Yes,'' she said glumly. ''Now there's even less motive. I haven't done anything to anybody.''

''Maybe you have something somebody wants. It could be that they weren't here to kill you but to rob you.''

''Look around, Gabriel. I don't have anything of value.''

''Well, one man's meat is another man's poison, dear. Just because you don't think something is valuable, doesn't mean that it isn't.''

''Right,'' she said. ''Actually, assuming that the killer was really here after me—for whatever reason—should make it easier to figure out who it is, shouldn't it? I mean, I must have done something to set him off and done it fairly recently.''

''You couldn't have done anything,'' Gabriel said. ''Not you.''

''But I must have, otherwise there'd be no reason for him to be after me.''

''Perhaps it was something . . .'' Gabriel appeared thoughtful. ''Have you done anything out of the ordinary lately? Gone anywhere new of late?''

''No. The only unusual thing I've done was to take a walk on the beach last Saturday night,'' she admitted. ''That's hardly something to kill someone over.''

''I should think not.'' Then he smiled. ''Not just a walk, Tess. You were diving for pearls quite far from the oyster bed, as I recall. And did you not sleep on the beach?''

"Yes, the dumbest thing I ever did. I'd rather forget that evening every happened.''

"Not I,'' he countered. "It was the night I met you, lass, and I'll never want to forget that.''

"Well, I guess I don't want to forget all of it,'' she admitted. "At least not your part of it.''

"Fate it was that took you there.'' He came to her and took both her hands in his and smiled at her warmly. "The same fate that has me lingering beside you.''

"I only wish you were lingering a bit more substantially. Oh, Gabriel, if I had a man like you...'' But she left the rest of her thought unspoken, feeling foolish having revealed as much as she had. She didn't mean to sound as though she felt he didn't exist, but in a way, he didn't.

"You've got me, of course,'' Gabriel said. "Though that does you no good, I'm sure. Tess, if my mission on this earth is to search the world over for a man who would treat you as you should be treated, I will do it gladly. Just ask me to begin looking.''

"You're too good to be believed,'' she said, looking up into his kind eyes. "Why can't you be real?''

"I'm as real as you want to believe,'' he whispered. "You make me feel as whole as I ever was.''

Gabriel brought his face down to hers still holding both of her hands in his, but then he hesitated, nearly frowning. Tess completed his movement, lifting her face to bring her lips into contact with his and give consent to the kiss. Gabriel released her hands, building that first shy kiss into another as he threw his arms around her and held her closely.

He lifted her, turning as they kissed, their lips suddenly at the center of the universe. Tess's body felt airy, as though she'd joined Gabriel's spectral realm in their contact. She felt as though she could fly and glide among the clouds fueled by the pirate's passion.

The touch of his strong hands sliding over her back and down across the denim covering her bottom sent a shiver through her as she'd never felt before. No man's hands had ever excited her as he did now, even though the fabric of her blouse and jeans were between them. No man's kiss had done this, ever, and she didn't want it to end. No, to remain like this would be more than she dared ask of life, and to die at this moment would be a perfect conclusion.

Whatever the doubts and fears in her life might be, now that she was in his arms, they seemed inconsequential. Here was a man who'd waited for centuries to hold her. He was here for her; she knew that. He had waited to love her; she longed to love him. They were perfect together.

The perfection was in their kiss.

When she opened her eyes slightly, Tess saw to her surprise that she had indeed been lifted up by his kiss. Her feet were at least six inches off the floor.

"I'm flying," she sighed against his lips. "You make me fly." Kissing him again, touching his broad, muscular back and clutching the fabric of his T-shirt in her eager fists, she wanted to soar even higher. "Lift me," she breathed. "Take me higher."

He said nothing, but leaned back and slipped a hand between them. He grasped her blouse and slid the top button free like a breeze, then the next and the next—until he was able to slide his lips down over the skin of her chest and kiss a pattern across her bra.

The night that had been approaching beyond the clouded sky descended while she was in his embrace, the last of the day's light slipping away, leaving them in the shadows.

"Come with me," Tess said breathlessly. "My room." And then her feet were on the floor again, leaving her to wonder if they'd really been drifting at all. "Wait," she continued, laughing. "Give me a second." She kissed Gabriel and hurried to her bedroom, eager to find a certain negligee, one she hadn't expected ever to wear again.

She should have known something was wrong because the bedroom window was open, but she noticed only a slight freshening of the air in the rain-scented breeze that entered the room. Only when she reached for the switch of her bedside lamp did she realize that she wasn't alone.

She smelled wine on his breath before he touched her. She turned—only to be thrown on her stomach on the bed. Her assailant pressed her face into the comforter to muffle any cry she might make.

Tess kicked and twisted against his hand, not thinking to cry out but only to escape the hand that held her and worked to twist one arm behind her back. And then something sharp nicked her wrist, and she did cry out.

"Gabriel!"

A clatter of movement greeted her call, a short yelp of pain and the pressure was off her back. Another yelp, followed by an inarticulate shout of alarm and confusion.

Tess rolled over and bounded to her feet just as Gabriel threw himself at a darkly clad man wearing a Halloween mask. The pirate's hands and arms were bare, so he had nothing to grasp or fight with, but his body was securely wrapped in its earthly wardrobe. He used himself like a battering ram against the intruder, slamming him against the wall and then against the frame of the window through which he'd entered.

The masked man's elbow shattered a pane of glass in the upper portion of the window as Gabriel struck him again, and then he twisted and dived through the window, hit the ground with a groan and ran away from the house.

"Are you all right?" Gabriel moved swiftly to her side and took her in his arms. "Did he harm you?"

"He cut my wrist, I think." Tess turned on the bedside lamp and leaned down, holding her forearm to the light.

A trickle of blood seeped from a thin cut on her wrist. It wasn't deep, for she hadn't allowed him a chance to do better, but it looked like a cut from a scalpel or razor blade.

"Does it hurt?"

"It stings a bit," she said, looking on the floor to see if he'd dropped his weapon. Yes, there it was, and she stooped to pick up a single-edged razor blade.

"Look at that!" she said, holding it up for Gabriel to see. "A razor blade!"

"Not a very good choice of weapon for a sneak attack," he observed.

"No, it's a perfect choice," Tess said. She didn't know the reason, but the method of this attack was clear. "He wanted to make it look like I took my own life! He was going to slash my wrists! Everyone would think I'd felt so guilty about killing Darrell that I couldn't bear to go on living. He wanted to turn me into a suicide!"

Only Gabriel's quick intervention had stopped the plan from working. Next time, she might not be as lucky.

Chapter Eleven

"You don't really expect me to believe this story, do you?"

Detective Sergeant Wilkes put his hands on his hips and looked at Tess as though he'd just uncovered an entirely new class of fool. She hadn't asked for him when she called 911 for fear of exactly this reaction, but he'd come anyway. And now she knew that Gabriel had been right when he'd counseled against calling the police.

"Yes," she said, "I do expect you to believe me, because it's the truth."

"Lady, you wouldn't know the truth if it bit you," Wilkes scoffed.

"What about the broken window and the footprints outside," she argued. "What about the razor blade and the pictures knocked down from the wall in my room? How do you account for that?"

"Oh, please, do I have to go through all the ways you screwed up when you fabricated the evidence?" he asked sarcastically.

She gasped. "Fabricated!"

"Yes, fabricated," he insisted. "First of all, anybody can buy a razor blade and knock a couple pictures off a wall. And you blew it with the window because it was obviously broken out, not in. If you break a window to get into some place, the glass will land on the floor inside, not in a flower bed."

"He didn't break it coming in! He did that in the fight!"

"The fight where you forcibly threw him out the window?"

"Yes."

"Stop insulting my intelligence. You didn't throw an intruder out of here any more than you threw your husband out before. You're lying."

"Is this attitude of yours just to compensate for the lousy search you did earlier?" Tess asked recklessly.

"You neglected to tell us that you weren't renting the garage," he said angrily. "You set us up to find the knife. You wanted to be certain it wasn't usable in court."

"I didn't know the knife was there and I didn't know it made any difference anyway," Tess insisted. "When will you people figure out that you're investigating the wrong person?"

"We're not," he said. "All we need is new proof."

"What about the footprints outside my window?"

"You put on a pair of men's shoes and faked it."

"So where are the shoes now? Search the house again if you want. Where are the man's muddy shoes that I'm supposed to have used?"

"You could have thrown them in the neighbor's trash. All I know is that you went to a K mart and purchased men's clothing on your way home this evening. A pair of shoes was among the items you bought."

"Oh, hell," Tess sighed. "You people haven't wasted any time in trying to make my life into a total disaster, have you?"

"Just quit trying to outmaneuver us, Miss Miller," Wilkes said smugly. "You're wasting everybody's time. We had a car passing here every five minutes and nobody saw anyone enter or leave the house after you came home."

"He came in through my bedroom window in the rear of the house," Tess insisted. "Of course you didn't see him."

"How very convenient for you. Now, if you'll excuse me, I'd like to get home."

"You're cheering the killer on, aren't you? You'd like nothing better than to find me dead, apparently by my own hand."

"No, I'd be disappointed. I'd rather convict you in court," he snapped. "Is that all you require of us tonight?"

"Yes, get the hell out of my house," she said. "And you can call off your blind surveillance team, too, because I'm going to bed now. I usually leave for work at about twenty of nine, so they can pick me up on their way from the doughnut shop."

"I'll run my own investigation, thank you." Wilkes turned and jerked his head toward the door. To the two uniformed officers that had come with him, he said, "Let's get out of here before she starts blaming Lee Harvey Oswald."

Tess clenched her teeth and remained silent. She knew that whatever she might say now, it would very likely land her back behind bars. And while jail might be safer, it was the last place she wanted—or needed—to be. No, she had to have her freedom to catch the man who was trying to kill her!

"Gabriel?"

"Yes, love," he said, stepping out from the kitchen. "I heard it all."

"Then you know we've got to find this man on our own."

"That I do," he said, smiling. "And I'll gladly break the scoundrel's neck for you, lass. See if I don't."

"No, don't do that. We need to catch him alive and able to talk," Tess said. "That's an absolute necessity. But first we've got to catch him."

Tess sat on the couch, leaning her head back against the cushions and staring at the ceiling. Gabriel sat beside her and playfully brushed the hair on her shoulder with a finger.

"You say you've made no enemies," he said reflectively.

"None. I mean, it would take a pretty serious grievance to lead to this."

"Aye, it would. So, what have you been witness to of late that would cause such hatred?"

"Nothing," she said with resignation.

"Come now, you must have seen something. Or at least been in a position where someone *thought* you saw something."

"We've been over that, and there's absolutely nothing. I haven't done anything or seen anything unusual. Except for meeting you, that is."

"Then it's back to your husband's business."

"But I had nothing to do with that except to sign a couple of papers. And," she added, sighing, "I signed everything back before the divorce. I don't have any claim to anything related to Cage Real Estate Development."

"Then it must relate to the beach this Saturday last."

"Why?"

"Because nobody tried to kill you before then, did they? And as you yourself said, you haven't done anything to set someone off like this."

"But I didn't see or do anything unusual that night, either. I was too busy trying not to drown."

"But the killer probably doesn't know that," he said.

"You may be right."

"You're being hounded for the sake of something you didn't see but perhaps might have."

"All right, then. I parked in the lot at Bernie's on the beach," Tess said. "Maybe something happened there. My car was in the lot overnight after all. If something happened there after hours, they might have tracked me down through my license plates."

"That's surely possible. Anything else?"

"No. I took a walk and went for a swim. You know what happened after that."

"Aye," he said, running the tip of his finger down her cheek.

"After you left me, I fell asleep. When I woke up, I went home."

"Nothing else?"

"No, nothing."

"When did you meet the moneylender?"

"Sunday morning. He came down from his house near the beach."

"So then it's the banker," Gabriel said.

"What? Oh, get real! He's a guy who gets by on his checkbook not his brawn. Hardly a murderer. And what could he have been doing that he didn't want me to see anyway?"

"That's what we'll have to find out on the morrow," Gabriel said. "Unless you'd like to call him on your speaking machine and ask him the question outright. I'm sure we could both do without the suspense."

"I'm sure not going to call him," Tess said. "Especially since he didn't do it. That would be insulting."

"Insulting? I'd say assaulting a woman in her home is a far greater insult."

"But it wasn't him."

"Well, I'll agree that bankers usually hire their dirty deeds done," Gabriel said. "But I believe him guilty of something."

Tess looked closely at the man then, noticing the furrowed brow above his noble green eyes. Though he was smiling, there was clearly tension in that face.

"Gabriel, are you jealous?"

"Me?" He frowned, then smiled. He caught the lobe of Tess's ear between his thumb and index finger and then tugged. "Aye, that I am. I hope with all of my heart that the man is guilty as sin, for he's the only competition I've got with you."

"I'll tell you a secret," she whispered. "He's no competition at all."

Tess kissed his cheek and snuggled her head against his chin as the secure feeling at his nearness grew within her again.

"Don't you ever go away," she murmured. "I'd rather die than lose you."

"I'm not leaving." He kissed the crown of her head, comforting her with a strong arm around her shoulders.

She could have sat like that forever, safe in his arms. It felt so good, and the pressures of the day seemed to melt away at his touch, leaving her to drift in the security of his strength until she fell peacefully asleep.

Gabriel carried her carefully to her bed, laid her down and covered her with the sheet. Then he lay beside her and watched her sleep, content just to be near her. Eventually, for the first time in centuries, he, too, fell soundly asleep.

WHILE TESS AND GABRIEL slumbered, the intricate knot of Darrell Cage's finances began to unravel at a faster pace. It began when Sergeant Wilkes returned to the station after Tess's call. He checked the report on the search of Darrell's office, which had been conducted by another unit that afternoon. Once he'd seen that, he hurried to the evidence locker to look at the material they'd brought in. Hours later, he was a bit more optimistic about his chances of nailing Tess Miller for the crime.

Jay Sturgis was working later than usual that night, too. In order to begin construction of a multimillion-dollar retail and entertainment complex between Tampa and Los Palmas, Carl Downey needed the key piece of beachfront property that Darrell had put into his wife's name. It was up to Jay to secure the property now, and he had to do it without bringing too much undue attention to bear on the acquisition.

Without the beach, the site lost its prime attraction; it was the reason for the majority of the rentals they had lined up to date. If Darrell had made Tess deed the property back to him before his untimely death, they would have had nothing to worry about. But now, Darrell's murder could bring any dealings between Tess Miller and Carl Downey under official scrutiny. In turn, that could slow them down—stop them entirely. They could miss their start date and the tax abatements Los Palmas had granted to get the project in town. That would mean lost revenue over the long run of the complex. But, even more importantly, a late start might mean defaulting on their completion bond with the bank. Timing was everything.

Jay wondered how much Carl had thought about the timing. It wouldn't be hard to imagine one of the other big construction companies who had been bidding for this land committing murder to keep Downey from succeeding. Jay could also imagine Carl Downey doing just that to keep the others in check.

He could only hope Carl wasn't mixed up in Darrell's murder. Jay could see no benefit to them, but it was possible that Carl had some broader scheme in mind. Or Cage might have been trying to up his share in the project and Carl just decided that it was better to be rid of him. Jay could only hope it wasn't so. As it was, they were only technically in violation of the law on this deal. Murder was far more than a technicality.

ACROSS TOWN, A MAN STOOD in the darkened living room of his tenth-floor hotel suite and finished changing the dressing on his badly gouged elbow. The cut was long and ragged but it wasn't terribly deep, so he had decided against stitches and had doctored himself with iodine and bandages. It seemed as though the wound had stopped bleeding. He'd be all right.

As he looked across town toward the ocean from his hotel window, he tried to piece together his experience that night. She'd been alone in the house; he was sure of that. It should have been a simple matter to subdue her and arrange for her "suicide." He had at least a forty-pound weight advantage, to say nothing of muscle, yet she'd thrown him like a linebacker.

He couldn't understand how that had happened. One moment she was beneath him struggling ineffectively, and the next she was pitching him against the wall. He wouldn't have believed it possible if he hadn't experienced it himself. And even more disturbing was his feeling of absolute helplessness during her attack. All he could think of was escaping and getting as far away from her as possible, and he hated himself for feeling like that.

She was only a woman after all.

It was just too bad that she was in his way on this deal. He didn't like the idea of killing a woman, but since the knife wasn't usable against her in court, he couldn't be sure that she would be convicted. The police might still come looking for him. He just couldn't afford to have any loose ends on this deal. There was too much money involved.

Of course, if he hadn't slipped one of the hotel steak knives into his pocket at dinner, he could have avoided this, too. It might have been embarrassing, but he probably could have talked himself out of a jam with the husband. That was nothing more than spilled milk now, and there was no sense regretting it.

He'd have another chance at the lovely Tess Miller. She was just a lone woman after all.

Chapter Twelve

Tess was conspicuously punctual in her arrival at work on Tuesday morning, but James Bentsen was in his own office, so he didn't see her entrance. She was uneasy at first, wondering just what the news reports had said about her last night and how much anybody here had seen.

Barb Davis reassured her immediately by greeting her with a big smile and saying, "So how's the jailbird this morning?" and laughing heartily. That seemed to break the ice, and both she and Juanita gathered around her to ask about the ordeal she'd been through.

"What about work?" Tess asked them. "Did they get through their meeting yesterday all right?"

"Not to hear Bentsen talk about it," Juanita said. "I swear that man would have a problem finding twenty bucks on the sidewalk. We didn't really need those numbers except to confirm verbal reports."

"But Bentsen likes to have paper in his hand," Barb returned. "I could have given him my grocery list."

"I'm not quite at six months yet, so I'm worried," Tess admitted. "They could save themselves from having to hand out a raise by letting me go right now."

"I hadn't thought of that," Juanita said. "But nobody mentioned anything about firing you. Of course, that was yesterday afternoon and you hadn't been on the news yet."

"The news reports didn't mention the company, did they?"

"Yes, I'm afraid they did," Barb said. "They described how you were picked up at work and everything."

"Oh, well, I guess all I can do is try to catch up on yesterday's work and see what happens," Tess said as she pulled her chair out from her desk.

"Miss Miller, would you come to my office?" James Bentsen called. "If you ladies are quite through chatting, that is."

Tess walked to the man's office and stood while he walked around his desk and sat.

"You may sit," he said.

Tess sat, determined not to apologize for yesterday's problems. It hadn't been her doing after all, and so she had no reason to make amends.

"Tess, you've been a good employee here," he acknowledged. "Very good with the books, but this business yesterday is...well, embarrassing to the company. Surely the investigation will be continuing for some months. Our directors have talked it over, and rather than take the risk that the good name of

Crowe Tool will be associated with a tawdry business like murder, we feel we must let you go.''

It was as simple as that—get in the news, lose your job.

"Mr. Bentsen, I—" Tess began angrily.

"I'm sure you wish an apology could make it all better. So do I, Miss Miller. But it won't. In business, your name is everything, and this will be bad for our name if we continue to be linked to the crime through the news media.''

"I wasn't about to apologize, Mr. Bentsen," Tess said. "I was only going to say that it's not fair that I be penalized for the police department's mistake.''

"No, I'm sure it isn't," he admitted. "But that is just the way it is. You understand, I'm sure, that this is a business decision, and it has nothing to do with you.''

"And nothing to do with my good work here," she said sourly.

"Excellent work, certainly. But the world is full of accountants, Miss Miller.''

"Yes," she said, standing. "Unfortunately, it's full of jerks, too. I assume that I'm through today?''

"Yes. You may take some time to clean out your desk, of course.''

"There's nothing in my desk," she snapped.

"Good. Well, then, have Juanita issue you a check for money owed and severance pay. Good luck, Miss Miller.'' He stood, extending his hand.

"Thank you," she said, ignoring his hand. "Goodbye.''

James Bentsen was wise to remain in his office after dismissing Tess, for the opinions expressed about him while Juanita wrote out Tess's check would have been alarming even for someone with his steely reserve. In the end, however, they agreed that no matter how unfair or inhumane it might be, Tess probably had no legal grounds to dispute him.

"Hey, ladies, what's happening here?" Betty Crown rushed up from the factory as Tess was folding her check into her pocketbook. "The rumor mill says Tess got canned. Is that true?"

"Yes, it's true," Tess told her friend.

"Bentsen can't do that," Betty declared, turning toward his office door. "I'll go tell that ignorant—"

"No." Tess stopped Betty's movement toward the manager's office by placing a hand on the woman's shoulder. "Why lose your job over mine? I'll be all right, Betty. Really."

"Sure you'll be fine," the other woman said. "But I'd still like to give him a piece of my mind since he obviously has so little of his own."

"He wouldn't know what to do with it," Tess said, laughing. "I'd better get out of here so you guys can go back to work. I'll stay in touch, don't you worry."

"I'll call you tonight," Betty said.

"Yes, that would be nice. No, wait. I've got that dinner date tonight," she said glumly. "I won't be home."

"You sure sound excited," Betty said. "Is the guy really that much of a slug? The news said he was paying your legal fees."

"No, he's not," Tess said firmly. "I'm taking care of that myself. And he's not really a slug. It's just that he's not my type."

"Well, get the free meal anyway," Betty advised. "Severance pay from this place isn't going to buy too many groceries."

WHEN TESS EMERGED in the parking lot, Gabriel said, "They sacked you? I would have expected as much. Well, that allows you the time you need to clear your name, doesn't it? Not to mention the small matter of bringing my treasure up. You've got too much afoot to bother with working."

"I like your attitude," she said.

Still, she felt glum about losing the job. Especially glum when she considered how hard it would be for a murder suspect to find new employment should Gabriel's grand vision of salvaging a fortune in a pirate's swag not come true. She left the parking lot feeling that one plan for her future, in which she'd invested over a year of her life, had come to nothing. Now she was back where she started in many respects.

Though not quite. After leaving Darrell, she hadn't gotten any severance pay. And she hadn't had a man, alive or dead, to rely on for help. For that matter, she didn't even have the promise of pirate treasure to hang her future on. When it came down to it, she was quite a bit better off than she had been.

Maybe Gabriel was right. Losing her job might prove to be the best thing that could have happened to her.

"YOUR INCORPORATION papers are filed and everything is ready to go, Charles."

Walter Chambers sliced into his steak and examined the meat briefly before bringing it to his mouth. He had been trying to watch his diet lately, so he was avoiding fat and ordering his steak cooked medium-well instead of rare as he liked it. He wasn't about to give up steak altogether, but he would do what he could to have a healthier life-style.

Now he was having an early lunch with Charles Dumont in the Holiday Inn downtown. The restaurant was excellent and the client was picking up the tab, so he was in a fine mood even if they did have to discuss business.

"I'd like to see Paul Driscoll in my office, however. There're a few matters we should clear up before everyone signs on the dotted line."

"I don't know if he'll be back in town before I have to leave," Charles said. He sipped his wine and watched the lawyer eat. He didn't like Walter Chambers very much—he was more honest than the lawyers Charles usually used—but he had been cheap and willing to step a bit outside of his area of expertise to set up the corporation. "Besides, he's already signed the papers."

"Sure, but we haven't," Chambers said, swallowing quickly. "You can lose a bundle if he pulls out of the deal. And he can, you know. No matter what a contract says, it can be broken."

"He's not going to pull out," Charles said. "If you have the papers, I'd like to sign them and get it over with."

"I've got them at my office. But as your lawyer, I'd advise you not to rush."

"I'm not rushing," Charles said impatiently. *Why didn't this man just take his share and run?* "But I have business to attend to, and I can't keep everything on hold while my nervous lawyer rereads a standard contract."

"You're the boss," Chambers said. He shrugged and cut into his steak again.

"What about Tess?" Charles asked him. "Is she in the clear?"

"No, she's in just as deep as before," the lawyer told him. "Deeper, really, because she's got the cops upset. Or I do, I suppose."

"They should learn to do their jobs better."

"Well, it looks like a dirty trick to them." He sliced another piece of steak. The lunchtime meetings were the best thing about working for Charles Dumont. "Of course, since they can't use the knife in court, they'll probably never get a conviction."

"Really?"

"Yeah, probably won't even take it to trial. I've been checking into Darrell Cage, and he was one shifty guy. Nothing really illegal, you know, but shifty. He was involved in an entertainment complex that's due to start construction next month. There was some nasty talk about how he obtained title to the property they'll be building on. He made a lot of enemies on that deal, and he had plenty to start with."

"He was a crook?"

"Not outright, but his partners sure are crooks." Chambers smiled. "I wouldn't hire Downey Construction to build anything for me if I wanted it to last. Of course, there again, it would be damn hard to prove anything about their building practices.''

''Well, Cage wasn't that smart. He was trying to make himself rich, but he wound up dead instead.'' Charles laughed. ''Bummer, eh?''

''Sure, but it's Tess's problem now,'' the lawyer said. He cut and chewed again. Then he paused, looking at the knife in front of him. There was something about the serrated blade and flat white handle that seemed familiar. He picked it up, turning it over in his hand. Yes, he'd seen a knife exactly like this somewhere else.

Where had that been?

BERNIE'S HAD ONLY BEEN open half an hour when Tess parked her car near the door and got out. She felt somewhat foolish. If people who knew she'd just lost her job saw her here, they would surely cluck their tongues in pity. They'd think she had gone directly to the bar with her final paycheck clutched tightly in her hand.

Almost directly, that is, for she'd stopped at home to put her bathing suit on beneath her jeans and blouse. She and Gabriel were going diving for treasure.

''So this is what passes for a tavern in these parts, is it?'' Gabriel said as he entered the large room invisibly at her side. ''An airy, bright place it is. Quite friendly. A switch from the establishments of my day, to be sure.''

"This is where I parked on Saturday night," she said, trying not to move her lips much, in case someone happened to be watching. "I don't recall witnessing anything strange. But then, I didn't even go inside."

"Well, then, we'll have to find the innkeeper to see if he knows of anything happening."

There were only three patrons at the bar, two of them sharing a table at the rear and one at the far end. As Tess walked through the lounge, the bartender stood up behind the bar. He'd been busy opening a box of cocktail napkins, and now he began filling napkin holders.

"Good morning," Tess said, taking a stool across from him.

He looked up and smiled. "Hi there. I didn't even hear you come in. What'll it be?"

"I just need some help."

"Everybody needs help. What kind of help did you have in mind?"

"A pint of stout would do for a start," Gabriel said in her ear.

Tess nudged the air next to her hoping to convince the spirit to be quiet.

"I was wondering if anything out of the ordinary happened in the bar last Saturday night. Were you working?"

"Not working, but I was here as a patron for some of the night," he said, leaning a bit closer.

"Did anything strange happen that night?" Tess repeated.

"No, nothing strange," he said after a moment's thought. "Unless you consider a complete lack of fights in the parking lot strange. It was a pretty slow night, really. You know, you look familiar. Do you ever come here?"

"I've never been in before," Tess answered. Great, people were already recognizing her from the news. "There were no disturbances at all?"

"No, not that I can think of. I mean, that was a couple days before they found Darrell Cage hacked up like that. Hey, that's why you look...you're Cage's wife!"

"*Ex*-wife," she said.

"That's for sure." He laughed. "So they arrested you and then kicked you back out again. I heard the cop screwed up the search."

"Yes, but that doesn't mean I'm guilty."

"Hell no, I didn't mean to make it sound like that. If you're here now, you must be innocent."

"Why?"

"Come on, why would you want to be seen out in public? I'll bet you've got cops following you every-where."

"Oh, yes, it's a big parade. Did you know Dar-rell? It sounded like you did."

"Oh, yeah, he held the title to my lot," he said.

"Your lot? What, your home?"

"No, the bar. I'm the owner. Sorry, I didn't intro-duce myself. Tommy Mott," he said, extending his hand. "This is my joint."

"Tess Miller." She shook his hand. "Why did Darrell hold your mortgage? He wasn't a banker."

"He bought up quite a bit of beachfront property," Tommy said. "I think he and some others were hoping to put that new hotel and entertainment complex down here, but they couldn't get the zoning changed."

"Hotel complex?"

"Yeah, they're building farther north instead. This area is zoned for residential use. They set the zone up around me 'cause I was already here."

"What happens to your mortgage now?"

"Oh, I suppose some bank will buy it. Anybody's better than Cage and Ventura."

"Cage and Ventura? I'm not familiar with that company," she admitted. "It wasn't Cage Real Estate that held the mortgage?"

"No. Cage and Ventura was the company I made the payments to. The sooner someone else buys my note the better."

"Why?"

"They're not so likely to foreclose and sell the property out from under me. Of course, I don't know about Ventura, but your husband was a real jerk."

"I know." She laughed. "So, nothing happened on Saturday."

"No. But I wasn't here all night."

"Ask about the neighborhood," Gabriel urged.

"What about outside the bar? On the beach or in the neighborhood, maybe?"

Tommy Mott thought for a moment. "No, nothing that I've heard of. Like I say, I did get out of here early."

"You're here every night? And then you work days here? Boy, you must love this place."

"Not really," the man said, smiling. "When you own it, you pay attention to it. Most of my help would just as soon sell everything out the back door as across the bar."

"What kind of neighborhood is this?"

"Rich and old, mostly. You've got to have bucks to get beachfront property."

"That's for sure. Well, thanks for your time, Tommy."

"Time spent talking to a pretty lady is never wasted," he said. "Sorry I couldn't help more."

"I didn't really expect that you could," she said. "Say, why is the place called Bernie's if a guy named Tommy owns it?"

"Bernie was four owners ago," the man said. "Nobody wants to pay for a new sign. It was called The Pirate's Lair before that."

"Really?" That seemed like an odd coincidence. "Why did they call it that?"

"Some sort of local legend, I think. There was supposed to have been a wreck out there someplace."

"I hadn't heard that," she said, her heart suddenly beating hollowly within her chest. "Do they know where?"

"No. It's probably not true anyway."

"You should give that man's motives a closer look, lass," Gabriel said in the parking lot a few minutes later.

"Tommy Mott? Why?"

"Your husband was his landlord and it was known that he had designs to sell the property. That's motive enough for any merchant."

"Except that Darrell was killed in my backyard."

"We can't rule out the possibility that Tommy Mott followed him there. And now that you're not locked up for the crime, he may have stopped by to put an end to police speculation."

"Him?" She glanced back at the bar, thinking of the affable bartender. She supposed anyone could be a suspect, though she couldn't picture Tommy as a murderer. "I don't know, Gabriel. After all, they weren't going to build that entertainment center here."

"So, your late husband may have been eager to dispose of the holding. You said yourself that he wasn't a banker. His business was in the selling of property, not owning."

"That's exactly what Darrell would have done," she admitted. "And he probably would have told Tommy that he was going to do it, too."

"Just keep an eye out for the innkeeper," Gabriel recommended. "Time will tell, lass."

"That's what I'm afraid of. And I wonder about this Cage and Ventura business, as well. Oh, Gabriel, there's too much to think about."

"Just think about one thing at a time and keep a watchful eye, lass."

"I'll try. Well, what do we do now?"

"We take a stroll along the beach, I think," Gabriel said. "We're very close to the spot where I went over the side, you know. I think we would best be served by heading to where you went swimming on Saturday.''

"What do you think about what Tommy said about the wreck? It could be your ship he talked about. Do you suppose anyone has looked for it?"

"Nobody as long as I've been here," he said. "And I've been here all the time. No, lass, the treasure is still where it landed, so we'll just go on a ways to measure the lay of the land. Then we should get a rowboat and do a bit of diving.''

"I'm not much of a diver," Tess said. "How deep is it?"

"Not more than thirty feet, I should say. It's buried under sand. I can take you straight to it," he said. "All we need is your hands to take hold and bring it up. You can do that much diving, can't you?"

"I've always wanted to be rich," Tess said. She laughed, rather liking the notion of being wealthy. "I guess I can stand to do a little work for it.''

WALTER CHAMBERS CALLED Tess's work number as soon as he got back to his office but was told that she no longer worked there. He smiled a tight, rueful smile. He had found out that Darrell Cage had secured the land on which Crowe Tool had recently expanded. Reports were that Cage might even have owned a piece of the company, too—hence Tess's being hired there with no work experience.

He dialed her home number next, nervously tapping his fingers on the desktop while he listened to the telephone ring twice, only to be answered by a machine.

"Tess, this is Walter Chambers," he said after the beep. "I've got new information. Your husband was into a lot of shady deals, and any one of them might have gotten him killed. You should take a look at any papers you might have access to and see what you can come up with. Also, I think I have something else. Maybe it's nothing. I don't know. But you'd better be very careful—"

The answering machine cut him off with a second beep. He began dialing the number again, nervously licking his lips as he did. But before Tess's message had ended, his office door opened and he quickly hung up the phone.

"Come in," he said. At that moment, he sincerely wished that he owned a handgun.

Chapter Thirteen

"This is where I stopped walking on Saturday night."

Tess stood beside the rocks again, this time in the hot, bright sun of midday. The gulf lay peaceful and calm, hardly a ripple disturbing its surface, and the air was heavy and humid. Tess had unbuttoned her blouse as they walked, tying it at her midriff over her swimsuit, attempting to let the air cool her as much as possible.

Only a handful of other people lingered on the pebbly sand today, but then this wasn't a tourist beach. Near Bernie's bar, families on vacation were searching for shells or wading in the blue gulf waters, but the line of houses overlooking this stretch of shore gave the clear impression of private property.

"Which one is the banker's house?" Gabriel asked.

"That one." Tess pointed to a two-story structure with wood-shingled siding and large windows overlooking the gulf. "I'm pretty sure that's the place he came out of."

"We'll have a look, then."

"Why?"

"He's as much a suspect in this matter as anybody."

"But, Gabriel, we can't just wander up there."

"Of course we can. He's a friend of yours, isn't he? There's surely no harm in calling on a friend." He kissed her neck from behind.

Tess flushed, then glanced around, wishing Gabriel was a flesh-and-blood presence, visible to all. "But he's not home now." Tess laughed, trying to push away the unseen kisses that now rained against her jaw. "Not during business hours. Gabriel, don't."

"So, if you get caught, you say you were mistaken, don't you? After all, you're newly unemployed and in search of a shoulder to cry on—or some such blather as that." He kissed her again, and one hand slipped across her stomach, visibly moving the fabric of her blouse while remaining unseen. "When would the best time to search a man's home be anyway?" he asked. "Not when he's at home, but when he's busy swindling people elsewhere."

"Okay, I get the point. Come on. But stop this kissing. People will see me and think I'm crazy."

"You're not, though. Only possessed by a spirit."

Tess walked up the gentle slope toward the house, the sand invading her shoes as it became finer and looser away from the water. A moment later, they were standing on a concrete patio. Above them, a balcony extended from the second floor.

"The least we can do is go around to the front, so we can pretend to be visiting." Tess headed for the side of the house. "We'll look suspicious if we're seen sneaking up from the beach like this."

"But you're simply taking a stroll along the water, aren't you?" Gabriel followed her to the front door. "It's not as though you have no explanation."

"I want a better one, that's all," she said. She stopped to read the number beside the front door. "Three Seventy-Nine Sandhook Road," Tess mused. "He really lucked into a nice place. These homes don't come up for sale very often."

"Try the door," Gabriel suggested.

"No way! I don't want to search Charles's house!"

"It's not that you don't want to, just that you don't want to get caught. Well, knock on the door or something while I have a bit of a look round, then."

"It's foolish to look. All we've got for motive is *your* jealousy of Charles. Gabriel? Gabriel, wait!"

But the pirate was already gone. He had decidedly entered the house in his own manner. Tess rang the doorbell and waited a moment as though she expected someone to answer.

"I don't think he's home!"

A woman's voice startled her. She turned and saw a gray-haired woman in shorts and a tank top, who was standing on the gently curving street.

"I wasn't sure if I'd catch him home during the day," Tess fibbed quickly, walking over to join the woman on the street. "But I was in the neighborhood."

"I haven't seen him since, oh, Friday, I suppose," the woman said. "Probably gone on a business trip."

"Yes, I guess so."

"Must have taken a taxi, though," she said. "Both of his cars are still in the garage." The woman had obviously taken a great interest in Charles's comings and goings if she'd bothered to peek through his garage windows.

"They are?"

"Yes, and that's strange since he normally just leaves his car in the lot when he flies. You a friend of his?"

"Yes," Tess said easily.

"Good for him," the woman said, smiling rather wickedly. "So young, too. Well, don't you be too rough on the poor man, young lady. 'Bye now."

"Goodbye."

Tess watched her walk away for a moment, then turned and looked up at the house again. What was she talking about? Was it some kind of neighborly joke? Charles didn't strike Tess as the type of man older women would joke with.

When she returned to the house this time, she took notice of the newspapers lying beside the door—one fat Sunday-morning paper and two each for Monday and Tuesday. She lifted the cover of the mail slot in the door and peered inside. Letters, flyers and magazines were scattered all over the entryway.

Why hadn't Charles attended to his mail? Was he deliberately leaving the impression that he was out of town? And if so, why? Tess was suddenly very curious. She wished Gabriel would return so that they could find a way for her to get inside.

Don't be a fool, Tess, she thought. *You have no reason to snoop around Charles's house.* But then she was supposed to go out to dinner with him tonight, wasn't she? If there was anything to be suspicious of, it would be best to know before the date.

She walked around the house again, trying unobtrusively to see into the windows. She looked into the garage as she passed between it and the house, too. There were indeed two cars inside. A moment later, she was on the patio overlooking the beach and peering through a large picture window.

The room, which appeared to be the living room, was tastefully furnished and quite tidy—except for a dirty glass. The glass contained a quarter inch of amber fluid and sat on a low table in front of a couch. Next to it was a plate with a half-eaten slice of toast. The food looked odd, left out like that. Tess didn't like the impression it gave her, but she couldn't be sure exactly why.

"Do you know of a man named Paul Driscoll?"

Gabriel's question startled her and she jumped back from the glass.

"Stop that!" she exclaimed. Then, catching her breath, she said, "Driscoll? The name sounds familiar...oh, I remember now. He's a businessman. Owns a couple of businesses, I think, though I'm not entirely sure. Why?"

"The man's name is on quite a few things inside the house," Gabriel replied. "And there are several small containers made of that plastic material you mentioned in his fancy upstairs privy. They have his name on their labels."

"Pill bottles?" she asked.

"Aye, I would guess as much. Is this Driscoll an elderly man that you know of?"

"I think so."

"Yes, the place has an old man's smell to it. And it's musty inside with nary a window open for air."

"Can you get me inside?" Tess asked now.

"I don't know if that's wise," he said. "If it's not your friend's house, you'll have no excuse for entering."

"But I could have sworn he said this was his house." Tess turned and looked at the beach. "There're the rocks where I sat down. I was swimming directly in front of this house and fell asleep on the sand there after you brought me up. I know for certain that Charles Dumont was coming from this house when he met me."

"Could he have committed some evil deed within these walls, where you might have chanced to see him?"

"Charles? No, of course not. But he did lead me to believe it was his house. I just want to look inside."

"No, I think we'll go about arranging to pay your lawyer instead," Gabriel insisted. "One thing at a time."

"Why are you suddenly so set against helping me inside?"

"I've given the matter more than my usual rash consideration and realize how it would look for you at this point in time," he explained. "The police are more than willing to suspect the worst of you already. It wouldn't do to be caught breaking and entering. Besides," he added, laughing, "I can't grip the door handles to open one up for you. We'd have to break a window to enter."

"I don't want to do that." Tess spoke in resignation as she watched the placid waters of the gulf lap languidly to shore. "Okay, so how far out do we have to go for your ill-gotten gains?" she asked.

"Out there, just to the south from where we're standing. Not half a mile from shore, I'd judge."

"If you were that close, why didn't they just run the ship aground and ride out the storm that way?"

"We could not come about to do it," he said. "The whole shoreline was different back then, and the wind was blowing at gale force. We would have gone over if the keel hit bottom."

"So they threw *you* over instead."

"Yes, thinking perhaps to call off the evil spirits they claimed were dogging our heels."

Tess stood a moment longer, just looking at the gulf. She knew that she should be more excited about the prospect of pirate treasure lying out there beneath the waves—especially now that Tommy Mott had given the idea more plausibility—but she couldn't muster very much enthusiasm for it. The treasure just represented money she needed to pay a lawyer. Beyond that, all she could see was a continuing investigation into Darrell's death.

Gabriel, on the other hand, seemed to be increasingly excited by the thought of regaining possession of his gold. He was speaking faster and with an almost musical lilt to his voice. But then, the sea was his life. For him, the gold represented the chance to regain what was taken from him by a superstitious crew.

Of course, Gabriel, or at least his spirit, was still alive, and Tess was beginning to wonder about the amulet. It had caused him so much trouble, and it was on the bottom of the gulf, too. Did the mysterious charm have anything to do with Gabriel's continued presence on earth?

And, if it did, could it be made to work its miracle once more with his ghostly form? Could it make him flesh and blood again? Now she realized that there *was* a reason to be excited about diving for the treasure.

"Where exactly did you drown, Gabriel?" she asked quietly.

"Why?"

"Your African necklace is down there, Gabriel," she said. "I want to find that, too."

"Do you think it's worth more than my satchel of gold and jewels?"

"No, but I'm beginning to wonder if that was what kept your spirit alive here," she said. "That might be why that native fellow was so eager to give it to you. He didn't want to die and turn into a ghost."

"I'll warrant you're probably right about that, lass. But it's already done its magic and so is no good to me now."

"But it might bring you back to life all the way. I know it's farfetched, but maybe it could give you physical form again. What do you think?"

"I wouldn't mind the chance to taste some of that food in your larder," he said. Then he laughed, saying, "But you might be a tad embarrassed to be associating with a naked man wearing a jewelled medallion on a thong around his neck."

"Don't be too sure," Tess answered with a grin. "I think a lot of people might envy me."

THERE WAS NO PLACE to rent boats on that part of the beach, but when they asked at Bernie's, they learned Tommy Mott had a small boat. He kept it in a storage shed behind the main building with volleyballs and other beach equipment.

"Still can't keep away from the scene of the crime?" he asked Tess as he unlocked the shed.

"No, this is a different matter," she said. "I'll keep track of the time and gasoline I use and reimburse you."

"No problem. How much could you use in an hour or two?" the man said. "If you really want to pay me, you'll tell me what this is all about."

"I will," she promised, "but later. Right now, I've got to go boating."

The skiff was made of aluminum and very light, with a five-horsepower engine. Hefting the gas container, Tommy said, "About half-full. Plenty of gasoline."

Then the two of them pulled the boat to a small dock and into the water easily. Once there, the bar owner connected the gas line to the engine and tugged on the starter cord. Three pulls did it. The engine roared to life and then settled down to a contented purr.

"You know how to run one of these things?"

"Yes, we used to have one at our cabin at the lake," Tess said. "It was years ago, but I see they haven't changed the design any."

"Then you're off," Tommy said. "At last I was able to be some help," he said. "Have fun!"

"We will," Tess said, waving.

"We? Have you got a mouse in your pocket?" he yelled. Then he waved, grinning. "Don't sink it!"

Tess waved back, grimacing at her unthinking use of the plural pronoun. Gabriel seemed undaunted by the slip, however, for he said, "You know, I thought him a bit of a cad, but he's quite a personable fellow after all. Let's give him a bit of gold in recompense for the boat, shall we?"

"It's your money," Tess said as she steered the craft farther away from the coastline. "But you'll have to direct me to it. I'd really like to find that medallion."

"Then take us north and a touch more out to sea," he directed. "We'll be toasting our success this nightfall."

Jay Sturgis brought the papers into Carl Downey's office at the construction company about the time Tess took command of the small boat from Tommy. He laid the papers on his boss's desk with a dissatisfied frown.

"I don't like any of this," he said.

"We've got to pay her," Carl said. He was smiling, looking at the papers with a satisfied air. "She's very likely to accept, now that she's unemployed."

"Yes, but if she checks into her husband's things before she signs, she's likely to find our connection to that penny-ante tool company. If she knows we got her fired, she's sure to stiff us on the price."

"And we'll pay it. That's all."

"But, Carl, we're hooked up with Cage and Ventura, too. Lord knows what dirty dealings of Darrell's could be connected to us through that."

"You worry too much, Jay," the older man said. "Take it one step at a time. Find her and buy the property. Nothing else matters right now."

"Meanwhile, if the cops start looking for someone else to blame for the murder, they could come up with us. Who killed him, Carl?"

"Do you really think I know?" Carl fixed the other man with a piercing gaze, clearly upset by the insinuation.

"I don't know," Jay said, flushing slightly. "But I don't want any surprises."

"Life would sure be dull without surprises, wouldn't it?"

CHARLES DUMONT had finished his business at the bank, setting up an account for the new corporation and depositing the money Paul Driscoll had given him before his suspicions had the better of him. Later today, he would write a check out to his other account at a different bank across town. In the morning, all of his deposits would be cleared and he could take the money out in cash in time for his 10:00 a.m. flight.

Temporarily at loose ends, he drove his car along Sandhook Road and past Driscoll's house just to be certain that there were no police cars parked outside, no telltale clumps of neighbors gathered on the curb to gossip.

He was relieved to see that the house was as he had left it, as still as a tomb. The neighborhood was very quiet. The home owners, mostly elderly people, were staying indoors out of the heat.

He continued along the street for a couple of blocks, then turned and drove past again. This time, he noticed a white sedan parked just south of Driscoll's house. Two men were seated in the vehicle, their attention turned toward the gulf. Charles knew instinctively that they were policemen.

So, there had been some official attention drawn to the area. But if they had discovered anything before now, they couldn't have kept the media from reporting it. And if they'd only just discovered something amiss, there would be considerably more official cars in evidence.

But those guys were cops, and they were watching something. What was it?

Charles continued driving. At Bernie's Lounge, he parked his car in the lot—and got his answer. Tess Miller's car was in the lot, too.

The cops were watching her. But where was she, and what was she doing?

Charles entered the bar and looked around. A couple of men were there, the bartender, but no women. No Tess Miller.

"Can I help you?" the bartender asked.

"Guess not," Charles said. "I saw a blue Toyota in the parking lot that looked like my buddy's car. Thought he might be in here. I guess I was wrong."

"Yeah, that Toyota belongs to a young woman," Tommy Mott told him. "She's out fishing or something."

"Fishing?"

"Yeah." Tommy shrugged. "Or something."

Charles thanked him and left the bar, smiling a bit at the idea of those cops sitting in their car watching Tess Miller fish.

So, what was she fishing for?

THE TWO POLICEMEN were wondering the same thing. They had been doing their duty with little interest all morning, both of them convinced that Tess wouldn't incriminate herself in their sight. They'd been more interested when she went to the big brown house and rang the bell, but no one had answered and she hadn't gone inside, so their curiosity hadn't lasted. But then she and Tommy had pulled out the boat and she had taken off in it. They got their binoculars and watched her travel along the coastline. She stopped, dropped anchor slightly north of their position and then began to dive.

"Better make a note of her location," the one in the driver's seat said. "Maybe she sank something out there."

"Like what?" The other officer didn't lower his binoculars. "The guy wasn't missing any body parts."

"I don't know," the first cop said impatiently. "Let's just see what she brings up."

They waited, watching the empty boat and catching occasional glimpses of Tess's head breaking the surface and going down again. Whatever she was doing, it wasn't normal. Maybe if they were real lucky, her activities would prove her to be guilty of murder. This might be all they needed to put her away.

Chapter Fourteen

The Gulf of Mexico was cold after the day's heat, and Tess shivered as she lowered herself slowly into it.

"Just let go and get it over with," Gabriel suggested. "It's better that way."

"No, it's not," she said. "You can't feel it, Gabriel, so don't start acting like some macho man."

He laughed at her scolding and Tess could see him floating on the water beside her without making a ripple.

"I should think the least you'd want to do is hide your body beneath the waves," he said. "I've never seen the equal of that swimming outfit of yours. It leaves nothing to the imagination at all, and surely it isn't keeping you warm."

"I'll bet you like it, though," Tess teased him. She released her grip on the boat and dropped the rest of the way into the water.

"That I do, but what I like or don't like is not the same as what a woman should be showing to the world at large," he chided.

"This is quite a modest swimsuit, Gabriel. You'll get used to it."

Gabriel allowed that he might well get used to it, but he certainly never wanted to take her for granted. No, he didn't want that to happen at all.

At a time marked by trouble, Tess found it liberating to be out on the gulf. She felt like a teenager on her summer vacation. As a teen, she had virtually lived in her bathing suit during the summer, and while she was married to Darrell, she'd never been a stranger to the sun. Now, of course, she saw the sunshine mostly through an office window. At least until this morning anyway.

Concentrating on the task at hand, she could almost believe that she hadn't a care in the world except to stay afloat in the peaceful waters. But she couldn't do that forever, either. If she wanted to dive, she'd better start before she became too tired.

"Okay," Tess said to her invisible partner. She pulled herself onto the side of the boat to reach for the diving goggles she'd purchased on her way to the beach. "I'm ready. Show me where it is."

She wet the goggles, then fitted them to her head.

"We're just above where I foolishly threw my treasure, Tess," he told her as he became visible to her at her side. "It was all in a leather satchel of fair size with a carrying strap and buckle to secure it."

"The leather is probably rotten by now," Tess said. She drifted out from the skiff a few feet, floating on her back and bringing her toes up to break the surface of the water. "The treasure is probably scattered over the floor of the gulf."

"Aye, it might be at that, but there'll be enough to pay for your lawyer and a couple months' lodging, I'll wager," he said. "Now, if you dive straight down, I'll guide you as best as I can."

"Here goes," Tess said. She slipped the goggles down over her eyes and took one deep breath, held it a moment and let it out. Then she took another lungful of air and flipped in the water, diving straight down.

She continued toward the bottom, her eyes on the shimmering panorama of brown and green. And as she swam, she felt Gabriel's hands gently on her back and the weight of his body slowly increasing, helping push her to the ocean floor. With his help, she was kneeling on the bottom in no time.

Gabriel remained nestled against her back, keeping her anchored while she dug past the water plants and through the loose sand and rocks. Even with his assistance, however, she found nothing. When she ran out of air, she pushed herself toward the wavering sunlight above them. Gabriel helped propel her.

"Nothing!" Tess exclaimed after she broke the surface and gulped in fresh air. "Is that the right place?"

"Yes, I'm sure of it," Gabriel said, floating at her side. "It's there, girl, I know it. It may be deeper or spread a bit thin, but it's there."

"All right." She dived again, Gabriel at her side, then once more dug into the bottom of the gulf.

Tess's fingers scraped across something hard and smooth, and she pulled it eagerly out of the sand, but it was only half of a clamshell, and she was forced to return to the surface empty-handed once again.

Her third dive was no more successful than the first two, and she was becoming winded from her exertions despite Gabriel's help. "One more time," she said, "then I take a little rest."

She dived again and shifted her search a foot down the slope from her previous efforts. This time, a couple of inches beneath the surface, she touched something rough and vaguely disk-shaped. She snatched it up quickly without even looking at it, but as the sand swirled away from her rising hand, she saw another dark object with roughly the same shape and texture. Tess grabbed this object, too, and pushed toward the surface.

She broke into the sunshine about ten feet from her anchored boat and swam strongly to it. After pulling herself up and in, she tossed her goggles aside and peered at the objects in her hand.

"What did you find, lass?" Gabriel asked.

"I think this is it," she told him excitedly.

At first glance, it appeared that she held nothing more than two rocks. They were both rough and black and nearly twice the size of silver dollars. Looking closer, however, she could see that the surface was rough, like a crust that had grown upon something rather than natural rock. She'd seen a documentary about sunken treasure on PBS, and this was exactly what coins looked like after centuries under salt water.

She tried scraping one of the objects against the side of the skiff without success. What could she use to crack the crust away?

"We should have thought to bring a hammer," she said. "I want to give these things a good whack."

"Bring up the anchor," Gabriel suggested. "It ought to carry the weight you need."

"Yes, that'll do it! Wait, won't we drift?" she asked worriedly. "I don't want to lose our position."

"Give me your shoe," Gabriel said.

"What?"

"I'll plant your shoe in the sand to mark the spot where you were digging," he explained. "And I'll keep an eye on the drift. Don't worry. We'll find it again."

"I hate to..." But it was foolish to worry about one soggy sneaker, wasn't it? "Okay, here."

Tess gave him her shoe and then hurried to the bow of the small boat and brought up the anchor. A moment later, she had the anchor in the boat, and as Gabriel looked on, she lifted and dropped it on one of the dark objects.

The anchor bounced away with a dull thud. A scattering of chips broke away from the object, leaving a black disk. Tess quickly grabbed the anchor again and used it like a hammer this time, hitting the black rock again and again.

She finally put her makeshift hammer aside to examine the find more closely. The fact that the object hadn't broken in two seemed to confirm her opinion, and when she brought it up to the light, she had all the proof she needed.

The crust of minerals had broken away from one side, revealing a flat surface that glowed with a dull sheen. A coat of arms was clearly stamped into it with something written below in what appeared to be Spanish.

"This is it," she sighed. "It's really an honest-to-God pirate treasure!"

"Did you think I was having sport with you, then?" Gabriel asked. "Of course that's what it is!"

"Yes, but, well, I never really expected to find it," Tess said. "I mean, people spend millions of dollars looking for something like this! I didn't expect just to dive down and pick it up!"

She stared at her companion in joy and wonder, wanting to hug him but knowing it would look very strange to anyone on shore.

"Well," Gabriel said, "I suppose there is quite a penny spent on such expeditions. But then those people don't have the owner to show them where it lies, do they now?"

"No, they don't at that," she said, staring at the coin. "This is quite a rush!"

"A thrill you mean?" He grinned at her. "Well, if you think this is a thrill, wait until I take you to the remains of the *Maria Louisa*. She was loaded with riches when I left her, and I suspect that she still is."

Tess threw her arms around him then, heedless of how strange it might look to anyone on shore. So what if they thought she was insane? She could afford to look a little crazy now.

Then Tess started the engine and followed Gabriel's directions back to the original spot from which they'd drifted and dropped anchor again. She jumped eagerly into the water and dived once more to the spot where her tennis shoe was jammed into the sand on the bottom.

She brought up six more coins on that dive and one more on the next. Then her discoveries compounded themselves when she found the remains of the leather satchel.

The leather was spongy and it stretched with the weight of its contents when she tried to pull it from the sand of the ocean bed. She dug quickly around it, managing to just get the tips of her fingers beneath it and pull it free.

It was heavy and nearly destroyed by time and salt water, but she managed to clasp it to her chest and push herself toward the surface, her lungs aching for air.

"Damn! This is heavy!" Tess exclaimed as she broke the surface near the skiff. "I—I can't lift it into the boat."

As she tried to maneuver the remains of the bag over the edge of the boat, she could feel a coin slip free and bounce along her leg into the depths.

"Oh, no, I'm losing it!"

"Here, I'll boost you," Gabriel said. "Hang on tightly."

Tess clutched the bag to her with both hands, leaning one shoulder against the boat as she kicked to stay afloat. Then she felt Gabriel's hands on her bottom. She was suddenly thrust from the water and into the boat, as the rotting leather gave way and spilled its centuries-old load.

Tess pulled herself up and swung her legs into the skiff. She panted and stared down at the treasure around her. These coins were not as badly encrusted with minerals as the first ones had been. Many still shone dully in the hot sun. And there were necklaces and other jewelry, too. Rubies and emeralds gleamed among the darker coins.

"How much did you have?" she asked Gabriel when he returned with her soggy shoe.

"More than that, but not so much," he said. "I would venture to say you've gotten the bulk of it."

"Good," she sighed. "I'm beat. It's an awfully long way down there."

"You'd best get to shore, then," he suggested, "and rest yourself."

"We've got to find your amulet first," Tess said.

"That can wait," he said. "It's not going any-where."

"Doesn't matter. I want to recover it now while I'm out here. Don't you want it?"

"Yes, but what if it doesn't work? The disap-pointment might kill me for good."

"I don't think so," she said, laughing. "But I know that *not* knowing will kill me. Come on, Gabriel."

"Well, then, we follow the coast north till we're abreast of that small spit of land that comes down to the water there." He pointed along the shore to an outcropping of rock, one just past the rocks where Tess had stopped walking the other night. "There," he said simply.

Tess pulled up the anchor and started the engine, taking them north along the coastline.

"NOW WHERE'S SHE GOING?" the driver of the police car said.

"Out for a cruise," the other cop replied. "What else has she got to do? She's unemployed."

"Yeah, must be hard on her, losing her job on top of everything else."

"My heart bleeds for her. She made mulch out of her husband with a steak knife, and you're worried about her job."

"She could be innocent. She sure doesn't act guilty."

"Innocent? I doubt it. She's just cruising around building up evidence for an insanity plea. She'll probably say she was treasure hunting."

"I suppose so. Come on, let's take a break. I've got to get out and walk around."

They drove off, leaving Tess and Gabriel to conclude their search without official scrutiny. The surveillance continued, however, for Charles Dumont had found a parking spot where he could see between the houses lining the shore. The rocky point where Tess was now diving had interfered with the shoreline and reduced the property value of that lot. Earlier, Charles had parked at the curb and walked down to sit near the rocks and watch. Now, with Tess approaching his vantage point, he scrambled back to his car to continue his vigil. He was seated directly opposite the spot where her boat was anchored.

"It's straight down from here," Gabriel told her once she was in the water. "I don't know what things will be like at the bottom. It could be difficult."

"I thought I would find, you know, bones or something," Tess said, grimacing at the thought.

"My bones are inside me, thank you." Gabriel laughed. "I'm no spirit, lass, though no man, neither."

"Oh, you're a man, all right," Tess affirmed, smiling. "And if I'm right about this amulet thing, we can make you even more of one."

"I'd like that," he said. "And then you and I will sample that barkeep's wares."

"It's a date. Well, here goes!"

Slipping her goggles firmly in place, Tess dived beneath the waves and descended with Gabriel's weight to help take her down.

The bottom was rockier here and it dropped off more quickly into a wavering field of undersea plants. After so many dives, Tess's head hurt from the pressure of the water above her, as well.

It was less likely for the amulet to be buried in this rocky terrain. Nevertheless, the multitude of shapes and colors hampered her search so that she was left to fumble around on the bottom while scanning farther afield for any sign of something auspicious.

She found nothing by hand in that initial search, and her lungs felt as though they would explode. But as she was about to push herself back toward the surface, she thought she saw a dull reddish glow farther down the slope. Had she really seen light reflecting from a polished surface?

Yes. It flashed again. Sunlight filtered down through the rippling surface of the ocean and bounced off something on the rocky bed. It was not a very bright red light. It could have been a trick of the refraction of the sunlight or an illusion created by Tess's oxygen-hungry brain. Tess moved toward it by grasping the swaying plants and pulling herself along.

Her lungs burned, and her limbs were tired and heavy, but she had to reach it now because she didn't want to dive again. When she got to the place, she found a black object with a fragment of rotten leather thong. There was no gem capable of making the reflection she'd seen, but she instinctively knew this was what she was after.

Tess grabbed the object—it was hot!—and she dropped it immediately. It fell, slithering farther down the slope as though actively trying to get away from her. Heat or no, she grabbed it again and pushed up as the ocean seemed to darken around her and her lungs ached to inhale something—even seawater.

She broke the surface with a convulsive gasp and used the last of her strength to swim to the side of the boat. She threw the object inside. Then she hung on to the boat, breathing deeply to gather the strength she would need to get back inside.

"Oh, God, I hope I'm done diving," she said. "I'm getting a headache, and my arms feel like rubber."

"Come on, into the boat," Gabriel said. "I'll help you in, lass, and you can rest proper."

"Is that it?" Tess asked as she let him push her up and then pulled herself the rest of the way into the boat. "There's a scrap of leather on it. A thong or strap, I think."

"Yes, that's the amulet," Gabriel said quietly.

He knelt beside it while Tess leaned her elbows on her knees and picked it up again.

It still felt hot, though not as hot as it had beneath the water, and Tess turned it over eagerly.

It was an egg-shaped piece with a face carved into either side. It was made of exceptionally hard wood or dark stone, which didn't seem to have been harmed at all by its time underwater. The features were cut broadly so that they blended into the zigzagging pattern that bordered it. In the center of the figure's forehead was set a dark red gemstone, much darker than any ruby Tess had ever seen. It, too, seemed untouched by time and it sparkled in the sun as she turned the amulet in her hand. Despite its size, the piece was quite light. It could be easily worn as a necklace.

"You were wearing this when they threw you off the ship?" Tess asked. She pulled at the scrap of leather caught in the hole at the top of the charm and it crumbled in her fingers.

"That I was," Gabriel said.

"You say the man who gave it to you was ill? Was he wounded?"

"I couldn't say," Gabriel told her. "It seemed that he was in the grip of a fever. I thought it was delirium that prompted him to want to part with so valuable an item. Now I see he was very clearheaded indeed."

"He was dying," Tess said. "He didn't want to linger after death."

"And so he gave it away to save himself."

"It sure looks that way."

The sea seemed terribly quiet then, and only the slight rocking of the boat broke the mood that overcame Tess as she looked at the charm in her hand. It was as though the world was put on hold while waiting for a decision to be made.

It was obvious to Tess that the previous owner had been afraid to die while in possession of the carved fetish. He'd given it to the first person willing to take it. It was also obvious that the natives who had taken the man had been unwilling to accept the gift.

But they knew the fate of its owner, didn't they? To live forever in a state of nonbeing was surely the worst thing to ever endure. Or could it be worse yet to take it back after death? Could there be more dire consequences?

"Give it to me," Gabriel said, making the decision for them. "I'll see if I can hold it."

Tess held it out to him in the palm of her hand. He reached over, and when his fingers touched the black wood, she felt the pressure of his touch. Smiling, Gabriel grasped the carving and held it tightly in his fist.

"It's hot," he whispered. "Oh, yes, I can feel the heat. And I can feel the boat beneath me, as well!" he exclaimed.

To emphasize the point, he struck his fist against the side of the boat with a hollow thump.

"I'm here," he said, "wholly here! Lord love it, I'm here once more! I—" His joyous expression changed suddenly to pain and horror and he stared at his fist. Smoke began to rise from between his fingers. "Oh, no!" he cried out.

As Tess watched in shock, the amulet seemed to burn through Gabriel's hand. Vainly, he tried to drop it. He held his hand open and shook it, but the amulet stuck to his flesh. His body glowed, and then flashed with a sudden flame that gave off no heat.

For a moment after the flash, Tess saw his skeleton blackened as if by fire, and then that was gone. The amulet dropped to the bottom of the boat.

"Gabriel!" she shouted. "Gabriel!"

But Tess was alone.

Chapter Fifteen

Tess was horror-struck. She sat staring at the space where Gabriel had been a moment before. "Gabriel," she whispered. There was no response.

"Gabriel Dyer!" she cried out.

Nothing.

And then she found herself weeping as though she'd always been crying. Great racking sobs shook her body as tears flooded over her cheeks. She brought her trembling hands to her face, wiping at the tears, but more flowed down in her sudden grief.

All she'd wanted to do was bring him fully to life, to make him as real as everyone else. She wanted to love him. She wanted to go out together in public and introduce him to her friends and simply have him at her side. Instead, she'd apparently brought on his final death. By reuniting him with the amulet that had originally kept his spirit alive, she had killed him as surely as if she'd shot him with a gun.

Had she been greedy? Was she asking for more than she could have by wanting him to be a live-and-flesh-and-blood man at her side? Was she destined to come that close and no closer to love? What had she done to be tortured so by fate?

Now she was all by herself, and having known Gabriel, she felt truly alone for the first time. The lack of his presence was a palpable hole within her now, something that she knew she would feel for the rest of her life.

Gabriel, what have I done to you?

She felt as though she might never stop crying, never stop grieving for the love that had almost come to life at her side. Now it didn't really matter if she were convicted of Darrell's murder or not, for she surely had nothing to live for.

But he had left her better off than before, hadn't he? He'd left her with the means to continue her fight to clear her name. And he wouldn't have her sit here mourning when there was still work to be done, would he? No, she could not imagine the intrepid Irishman weeping like a baby. No matter what he felt, how much he might be torn up inside, he could carry on with his life. He would overcome his grief rather than give in to it.

She knew, too, that he would expect the same of her. A man who held on to life as tenaciously as he had would have no patience for anyone who chose to spend their life grieving. Tess wasn't about to dishonor his memory by acting like a fool out here on the gulf. She would do her mourning later, in private.

"Okay," she said to herself. "One thing at a time, right? Tackle each problem as it comes up. Right now, you've got to get back to shore and figure out how to turn these jewels and antique money into real cash.

You've got to pay your lawyer if you want to stay out of jail.''

The sound of her own voice calmed her, allowing her to concentrate on her task enough to get on with it. She pulled the anchor up and then started the engine. The cool air rushing over her face as she sped back toward the shore dried her tears. It almost made her feel like a sailor facing the ocean waves as Gabriel had done in his life, and with that feeling, she was able to achieve a kind of closeness with his memory.

For a moment, the thought of Gabriel brought fresh tears to her eyes, but she brushed them away and set her jaw with determination. Later, she promised herself, she would mourn him later.

Of course, she didn't have a clue how to go about dealing with the coins and gems. There were probably legal formalities to go through—claims to make on the treasure. It looked as if she would need her lawyer for more than a criminal defense.

Walter Chambers was probably the man she needed to see next. Yes, she would visit him and ask for advice on how to convert the treasure into cash and protect her interests in the find. After all, she had more claim to it than anyone. One of the owners had given her that claim.

Tess piloted the boat back to Tommy's bar, got out and tied up at the dock. Then she slipped her blouse over her swimsuit. She stuffed her slacks into the plastic bag from the store where she had purchased the goggles. She used her straw tote bag to hold the jewelry and encrusted coins, for the leather bag was beyond any use now.

After she'd scooped the coins and jewelry into the tote, she picked up the amulet from the floor of the skiff where Gabriel had dropped it. Her first impulse was to throw it back into the sea, but as she clasped it, the warmth it gave off stopped her, and she stood looking down at her clenched hand.

The carved charm was definitely warm and it seemed to grow hotter within her closed fingers. She wasn't worried about suffering the same fate as Gabriel, but the thing was becoming increasingly uncomfortable to hold. Finally, she opened her hand and let it rest on her flat palm.

The heat immediately dissipated into the air.

Something made her keep the token. She thought that if its heat could ebb and flow like that, its effect on Gabriel might also come and go. There was a possibility, though a slim one, that she still might need this magic carving, and she slipped it into the tote along with the rest of the treasure.

CHARLES DUMONT was confused by Tess's activities in the gulf until he saw her bring something up from the ocean floor. Then, though he didn't know what she'd dropped into the boat, he felt reasonably certain that it involved money in some way. Why else would anyone go to so much trouble? Maybe he should have checked her background more carefully. But it didn't really matter, did it? Anything she'd be willing to hide beneath salt water couldn't be worth much money, could it?

When he saw a man appear out of thin air on the boat and shout something that was carried away on the breeze, his interest was piqued. Charles knew he wasn't hallucinating. He saw the man blink into existence as clearly as he could see Tess's boat. And then he saw the man burst into flame and disappear again as some small object flew out of his grasp.

Now that was something worth looking into.

TOMMY MOTT WAS BEHIND the bar when Tess entered. There were no customers and he was working on a crossword puzzle in the paper.

"Hey, done fishing?" he called out when she entered.

"All done. I'll help you put your boat away," she said.

"No problem. I'll get it later. Any luck?"

"Yes, some," she said without much enthusiasm. "Where's your ladies' room? I have to get out of this wet suit."

"Right over there," he said, pointing. "Can I interest you in a soft drink? Orange juice?"

"No, I...well, I guess a glass of orange juice would go good right now. I'll be right out."

Tess changed quickly, putting her wet bathing suit into the bag with the goggles. She paused a moment, studying her face in the mirror. Her lip trembled a bit, but she clenched her teeth and then washed away the traces of her tears. She left the rest room determined to put the best face possible on things.

"You must have found quite a load of shells," Tommy said when she returned to the bar.

"What?"

"Well, that bag looks pretty heavy," he said. "I figured you were looking for shells to sell to curio shops."

"Yes, well, not exactly."

Tess regarded the bar owner thoughtfully. Gabriel had warned her not to trust him at first, but then he'd changed his mind. What would he say now? Would he trust the smiling bartender? She thought that his counsel would be to trust her own instincts on the matter, and she now felt she could trust Tommy. If Gabriel was indeed gone, she would need more than just a lawyer to help her.

"Do you have a safe here?" she asked as she drank some of the orange juice he'd set out for her.

"Sure. Two of them. There's one in my office and a drop safe out here."

"Good. Listen, Tommy, how are you on keeping secrets?" she asked.

"Okay, I guess," he said. "I did snitch on my older brother once when he broke a window, but he taught me how to keep a secret after that. Why?"

"I don't know. I think I need a partner, though I don't know for sure."

"A partner in what?" He smiled broadly, obviously expecting some kind of joke. "I don't have any money to loan you."

"I don't need a loan. Actually, I'd like to make a payment." Tess hefted her tote bag onto the bar and looked inside to select an item and bring it out. "I would like to pay you for the use of the boat and rent space in your office safe," she said. "I'm going to trust you because I have no one else to trust."

"That's as good a reason as any, I suppose," Tommy said. "What's the gag here?"

She placed a necklace on the bar before her. It was a gold chain, blackened by time, with four gems that appeared to be emeralds.

Tommy looked down at the bar, then quickly picked up the necklace and looked at it. His eyes widened. He turned the piece in the light. "You, ah, you weren't exactly collecting shells, were you?"

"No, I wasn't."

"My God," he whispered. "This is how you pay for a boat? With a necklace that's probably worth thousands of dollars?"

"I need a partner, Tommy. I can't haul this stuff downtown to my safe-deposit box, and it probably wouldn't fit anyway. I sure as hell can't hide it at my house."

"No, that might be a problem," he admitted. "But why a partner? I mean, if that bag is full of stuff like this, then we're talking about a whole lot of money. Why do you want to cut me in on it?"

"Because I need time and I need help," she said. "It'll likely take a couple of weeks just to convert this into cash. I don't know where I stand legally, Tommy. I may need to stake some sort of claim."

"I know some people who could probably cash something like this for you without going public," he offered.

"No, I want it all legal," she insisted. "Taxes, fees, whatever. This bag is just the start of it."

"What do you mean?"

"You remember telling me about the shipwreck? Well, it's not a legend. It's true, and it's out there. I just need time to find it and lay claim to it. I know that word of a sunken pirate ship offshore here would probably help your business quite a bit, so I'm asking you to keep it under your hat. Don't tell anyone anything about me except that I borrowed your boat and brought it back a few hours later. I don't want cops or reporters or anyone to know about this until I have clear legal title to the wreck."

"Fair enough." He extended his hand to shake hers. "You've got yourself a partner. Now get yourself a good lawyer and call the state."

"I've got a lawyer who can probably help." She took out several coins and laid them on the bar. "I wonder what's the best way to clean this crust off the coins?"

"Try vinegar," he suggested, examining one of the coins. "Soak them in it till the crust comes off. That works with coins folks find along the beach with metal detectors. Of course, those are modern coins and they haven't been in the water so long."

"It will probably work for these, too," she said. "See, you've helped me already."

"Worth every cent, too, huh?" he joked, giving her back the coin.

"Yes, every cent. I'd better go talk to my lawyer."

"Uh, before you leave, I should tell you what I already know," Tommy said. "More than likely you're going after the *Maria Louisa*. That would be, ah, don't tell me...Dyer," he said. "Gabriel Dyer's ship."

"Yes, how did you know?" she asked in surprise.

"I grew up here," he said. "Playing pirate was one of our favorite games when we were kids. There's a finger of land sticking out of the beach north of here that they used to call Dyer Point."

"Yes, that's near where I found this."

"Boy, I guess that stuff I read about it was true. And to bring up a haul like this without equipment is fantastic. You must have had damn good directions."

"What do you know about the *Maria Louisa?*" Tess asked, steering the conversation away from the topic of her source of information.

"She went down in a hurricane," he said. "That's common knowledge. Though it's always been assumed that she was several miles out to sea. About the middle of the gulf. That's obviously not the case, is it?"

"No. But how did anyone know about Captain Dyer? I thought all hands went down with the ship."

"A couple of the crew got to shore and settled here. The crew was mostly Spanish. They said the ship was loaded to the gills with loot. But then they said they were miles out, too. Neither one of them lived long but their story got around. I came across it in a local history book when I was a kid. Apparently, this Dyer was bad luck. Something about witchcraft. It wasn't very clear in the book, but it seems they tossed him overboard trying to get the storm off their backs."

"Didn't anyone ever look for the ship?"

"Yeah, some guy in the mid-sixties, but way out in the gulf. He never found anything."

"Do you know anything else about Captain Dyer?"

"The stuff I read said he was a wild man. He stranded the captain with the help of some crew members and took over as captain. They never had a moment of luck after that and eventually went down. Of course," he added, grinning, "that story came from two of the people who threw him over the side. It's probably a bit exaggerated."

"Probably." Tess laughed. It was strange to hear this about a man she'd just been talking to. A man who...no, she wouldn't think of that. "I didn't know any of this," she said quickly.

"I bet the books are still in the library," he said. "I sure did love this stuff when I was a kid."

"Do they still call that part of the beach Dyer Point?"

"No, they just complain about how it ruins the beach. The state won't let them change the configuration of rocks there, though. It helps protect the coastline."

"It's lucky they didn't take it out," she said, hefting her bag again, "or I wouldn't have found this."

"How'd you find it at all if you didn't know any of this?"

"Just lucky," she said. "I'd better go now."

"Right, you take care of your business," he said. "I'll hang on to the booty. Here—" he brought a small box out from behind the bar "—dump the stuff in this so you can take your purse out with you. You don't want the cops noticing that you left it."

"Good idea. I knew I needed a partner." She did as he suggested, slipping a few coins into her pocket along with the amulet, and then she packed her bag with the goggles and bathing suit into the straw tote. "Okay, I'll be in touch."

Tess left the man happily humming to himself as he polished his bar and dreamed of gold doubloons.

WALTER CHAMBERS'S law office was not exactly in the most prestigious part of town. Though she wouldn't quite describe it as run-down, his neighborhood had a definite low-rent feel to it. His office was on the second floor of what was apparently a renovated motel three blocks from the ocean. The newer hotels closer to the beach had drawn the business away, leaving this example of fifties architecture to find new uses. It had done so by providing office space for debt collection agencies, unsuccessful lawyers and other, less savory, businesses. The building itself was well kept, however, with a fairly new coat of paint and potted plants along the sidewalk in front.

Tess parked and hurried up the steps leading to the north end of the balcony and to the door bearing the number on Chambers's business card. Then she went inside.

The reception room was small. A secretary's desk and three padded chairs were in front of the picture window. No one was there.

"Hello?" she called out.

No reply.

The door to the side of the desk was slightly ajar, as though someone had pulled it shut on the way out and it hadn't latched. Walter Chambers didn't strike her as a man who didn't close doors behind him, and he surely wouldn't leave his office unlocked if it was empty. Tess assumed that he had stepped out for a moment and would be back soon.

She sat on one of the chairs by the window, picked up a magazine and thumbed through it for a couple of minutes. Nobody returned to the office, and after five minutes, Tess began to feel very uneasy. In fact, she began to feel that she should get out of the lawyer's office right away.

Feeling sudden panic, Tess stood and opened the door leading out. Then she stopped herself and took a deep breath. No, she shouldn't go without leaving a message of some kind. She turned back toward the office. Then she frowned. She didn't want to leave it here for the secretary—or anyone else who wandered into the unlocked reception room to see. No, she would leave it on Chambers's desk.

Tess strode quickly to his office door, pushed it open and stepped inside, only to find herself standing across the desk from her lawyer.

She froze, caught by Walter Chambers's sightless gaze. The lawyer whom she had come to rely on was beyond helping anyone now. The slash across his throat guaranteed that.

The office was silent, the traffic noises and even the sound of her own breathing seemingly sucked into the same void into which Walter Chambers's life had gone. It was as if all sound and sensation was absorbed by the dark red blood that stained the lawyer's shirt.

And as she stared at him, her breath caught painfully in her throat. She knew with deadly certainty that Darrell's murder, the attack at her home and her lawyer's grisly death were linked. Just as she knew that the murderer would not be satisfied until he'd completed the chain of deaths with her own.

Chapter Sixteen

Walter Chambers sat slightly slouched, his eyelids drooping, as though he were half-asleep in his chair. Only the cut across his throat and the blood disturbed the apparent tranquillity of his posture.

Tess wanted to run from the room and try to pretend she'd never gone there. She wanted to hide beneath the covers of her bed, to sleep and to see if in slumber she might be able to turn it all into a dream. But she knew she couldn't do that; she knew running wouldn't help her now.

If only Gabriel were here.

But he wasn't, and she had only her own wits to rely on.

Once she had taken a moment to collect her thoughts, Tess's mind seemed to become more clear in adversity, and her initial panic ebbed as she considered her options. She had very few.

She noted, with rather detached clarity, that she was standing just inside the door wearing the sneakers she had worn on the beach. She was probably leaving telltale grains of sand that could be used to link her to the crime. One of her sneakers was still wet, which meant she was leaving further evidence with each step.

She could not remember everything she had touched in the office to this point, but she felt she must have touched everything. And since she'd never been to the office before today, even a single fingerprint could be incriminating. She felt as though even the exhalations of her breath would leave some sign the police could use to link her to this murder.

Besides, if the police were following her as they had promised, there was a good chance they'd seen her come in here.

No, it wouldn't be wise to erase the signs of her visit, so the only thing to do was to make good use of her presence now that she was. But how could she do that?

Tess took another step into the room and forced herself to look at the papers on top of the desk in front of the lawyer's body. Blood had spattered all over the surface. It was quite dry now, however.

Walking around to the side of the desk, Tess tried to read the papers without touching anything. It looked like lots of legal mumbo jumbo. Even if the papers pertained to his death, Tess didn't have the background to understand them.

Looking around the room, Tess couldn't find much else to help her, either. The file drawers were all closed, and she wasn't about to open any of them to look inside. Aside from those on the desk, no other papers were visible. There was nothing to indicate who had done this or why. Maybe there was nothing to be gained by staying. She should get out now.

Then she saw that the lawyer's Rolodex file was open to the *D* section, the name "Driscoll, Paul" exposed. Tess looked at the card and suddenly recognized not the name, but the address—379 Sandhook Road.

It was the address of the house Charles Dumont had apparently come from when she'd met him on the beach. It was the house Gabriel had wanted her to search earlier in the day. And then she remembered the name, as well.

Had Charles bought the house from this Paul Driscoll? Had Walter Chambers helped him with the purchase? Maybe that was how they'd met. After all, it was clear from his office that Walter Chambers wasn't exactly the type of high-priced lawyer whom she might have expected a banker of Charles's stature to use.

She knew now that her only possible next move was to return to that house and find a way to get inside. That's where the answer had to lie!

But first she had to make her way out of the building without arousing suspicion.

She pulled the lawyer's door shut with the toe of her dry sneaker, then peered out the front window of the reception room into the parking lot. For nearly five minutes, she searched for police vehicles or passersby who might identify her later.

One person left the building and drove off in a late-model sedan, but she saw no one else. As far as she could see, the cars parked below her were unoccupied. The coast was clear.

Tess used the tail of her blouse to grasp the knob of the outer door and was just turning it when she paused, looking back at the secretary's desk. There was one more thing to check before she could leave.

She hurried to the desk, stood behind it and studied the tidy arrangement of items upon it. In the upper left-hand corner sat a daily appointment calendar, the pages separated into lines for each hour of the workday and designed to be flipped over on twin metal rings.

Tess noticed immediately that the calendar was already turned to the next day's page. The lawyer had appointments with two people in the morning and one in the afternoon and another to visit his dentist at three. She pulled a tissue from a box on the desk and used it to cover her fingers while she flipped the page over for today's schedule.

But that page was for yesterday. Someone had removed today's sheet from the calendar! Her hopes of finding out who was scheduled to meet with Walter Chambers today had been dashed!

Tess scowled, then she flipped back several pages to find that Charles Dumont had met with him on Friday morning at ten and Thursday at two. There was also a notation for an afternoon meeting a week ago Monday, but it had an additional jotting penciled at an angle in the margin. Tess tilted her head to read the words, feeling an odd mixture of fear and elation at the same time.

Beside Charles Dumont's name was written ''Driscoll deal,'' in a light, feminine hand. That confirmed the connection between Charles and Paul Driscoll.

The "deal" referred to was probably the purchase of the house on Sandhook Road. After all, Charles hadn't said how long he'd been in residence there.

She had to think things over. She couldn't do that here, so she turned the pages back to where she'd found them and then hurried to the door. Once again, she used the tissue in her hand to turn the knob, and pull the door shut behind her. Then, moving as casually as she could, Tess walked along the length of the balcony and headed downstairs to the parking lot and her car.

"Miss Miller?" a man called to her just as she slipped the key into the ignition. Tess jumped and grasped the wheel with convulsive force. "Miss Miller?" the man repeated.

She turned. A dark-haired man leaned over and looked in at her through the window. He didn't look like a cop; maybe she was all right.

"What?"

"Had a hard time tracking you down," the man said. "I'm Jay Sturgis. I represent a party interested in purchasing some property you own. We had contracted to buy it from your husband before he died only to find that you hold title to it. Could we go somewhere and talk about it?"

"No," she said quickly. "I don't have title to any property, Mr. Sturgis. Not anymore. I've got to go now."

"Well, we need to make an arrangement quickly, miss," he insisted. "We're willing to pay a fair price."

"How much?"

"One hundred thousand dollars." He smiled like a used-car salesman making an offer that was really too good to be true. "Fair enough, I think."

"I'll think about it," she said. "Goodbye."

Tess put the car in gear and drove off, leaving the man no choice but to step back and watch her drive away. Only when she was in traffic and headed home did she allow a shudder of fear to betray her tension. That was too close for comfort.

She knew she should have gotten more information from that Sturgis fellow, but she couldn't bear to stay in the lot a moment longer. Now she could only wonder what he was talking about. She had signed all the papers Darrell had given her. None of his little tax dodges had been missed, and he had regained title to all the business property and real estate he'd put in her name. What on earth could that man have been talking about?

As she drove, another thought occurred to her. What if Darrell had made some kind of deal with that man but had held out in some way by leaving a key piece of real estate in Tess's name? It wasn't unthinkable that he might do something like that. He'd play any angle he could think of to make a dollar.

What if the man had found out about the scam? What if he'd decided to do something permanent about Darrell. And what if he thought Tess had been in on it with her ex-husband?

What if?

Maybe it was time that she took steps to find out more about Darrell Cage's business affairs.

"SHE MUST KNOW WHAT we're after."

Jay Sturgis dropped the folder of papers on Carl Downey's desk and sat heavily across from the older man. "She wouldn't even talk to me."

"You told her our price?"

"Yes, but it was no deal."

Carl scowled and looked out the window for a moment, then he turned back toward his assistant and said, "Well, you did your best."

"We could offer another twenty thousand," Jay suggested. "Hell, we could double the price and still come out ahead."

"No, she'd see right through that. Nobody doubles their offer, Jay. You say she wouldn't talk—even for a hundred grand?"

"No, just drove away."

"Well, you did your best," Carl repeated. "Leave the papers with me and go on home."

"But, sir, we've got to convince her."

"Yes, we do," Carl said stonily. "Go home, Jay."

Jay Sturgis started to say something but stopped himself. Carl Downey hadn't gotten where he was in the construction business by taking no for an answer, and his tone left no room for doubt that it was in Jay's best interest to go home and have nothing to do with anything else at the office this evening.

"Good night, Carl," he said.

"Good night." Carl remained immobile in his chair until the door had closed behind Jay, then he picked up the phone and dialed a three-digit extension number. "Okay," he said into the receiver. "Go to it."

After hanging up the phone, he left the office and went out to an early dinner in a very public place.

TESS DROVE UP TO Darrell's house with a sense of trepidation filling her heart. These three acres surrounded by a low stucco wall had been her home once. The white Art Deco house was where she had hoped to build a home with the man who had seemed so wonderful. There were too many memories here.

Of course, that was all before she'd met Gabriel Dyer. *Oh, Gabriel*. What was she going to do? She had to get him back!

But now, she had to look for clues. She approached Darrell's estate beneath a canopy of thickening gray clouds, determined to find an explanation for the man's puzzling offer.

Despite the divorce, Darrell had insisted that she keep a key as well as a remote control for the front gate and garage. Now she was glad she'd done so, and she used the remote to open the gate, then drove up to the house. She didn't know what her legal status was or whether she was entitled to come here or not, but she felt she had as much right as anyone, no matter what she thought about Darrell. The police would probably be perfectly happy to have her poking around in Darrell's things in the hope that she might do something to incriminate herself in his murder.

Well, there was little likelihood of that. But if the cops hadn't taken everything away, and if they hadn't searched his house as thoroughly as they had hers, she just might find something. She might even find a motive for someone else to have killed Darrell Cage.

See, Gabriel? I'm not giving up. I'm not licked yet.

But even as she thought about the stalwart pirate, she couldn't help the feeling of pain and loneliness that welled up within her. What had become of Gabriel Dyer?

GABRIEL'S FIRST real sensations in over three hundred years were too brief and confused to be sorted out at once. The feeling of the solid boat beneath his feet and the sun on his back. The rocking motion of the light waves and the cool gulf breeze. The smells of the ocean and of the lotion Tess wore. All these things struck him at the same time, as though the touch of the amulet had been a gong rousing him out of a deep slumber. He exulted in the feelings, the remembered but yet brand-new feelings of life within his own body. He rejoiced.

And then the fire struck his hand and engulfed him before he had a chance to react. The fire burned him as no fire ever had, scalded his very soul with ancient magic so strong that it overcame his body and the world around him, overcame his life once more.

He was in darkness.

He was lost to the world that so briefly claimed him.

But he was aware, and in that awareness came the realization that he was as he had been before. The amulet hadn't killed him, though he imagined Tess thought so. No, it hadn't killed him, but he'd obviously done something wrong in using it and now he was as good as dead when it came to helping Tess.

In the darkness, he floated as if in a stupor for an uncounted period of time, drifting away from the pain that had consumed him and separated him from his love.

Eventually, the world came slowly back. It was as though a black fog was lifting away from it. The green of the ocean and blue of the sky washed in from behind the darkness to engulf him in new colors—the colors of life just beyond his reach.

And the world of a timeless ocean surrounded him and soothed him with its rhythm even as it taunted him with reminders of the life that had almost been his. The brief touch he'd had was enough to make him burn with desire for more, and that emotion was the only feeling allowed him in his eternal home beneath the waves where he'd died.

Where was Tess, and how could he tell her not to give up hope for him yet? How could he help her now?

How, indeed?

TESS HAD BEEN SURPRISED that there was so little evidence of the police investigation at Darrell's house. There were no yellow tapes across doors warning people to keep out, no padlocks or warning signs. She'd expected at least that much. But then, the house hadn't been a crime scene, had it? And though she hoped not, she now expected they'd taken away anything of any possible use.

But Tess knew Darrell Cage better than the police did, and she knew that what he'd left out for public scrutiny would only be the tip of the iceberg. Darrell was a grasping, manipulative man, and he wouldn't allow all his assets to be known if he could help it. No, he'd wanted to hold on to his possessions too badly for that.

Tess had entered the house and hurried through the spacious living room, where the white walls and light oak floor seemed to amplify the gray light filtering through a skylight. Beyond that lay Darrell's home office, a square room facing the ocean, with a beamed ceiling and oak wainscoting. It was there that an official presence became known.

His file drawers were open and empty; the drawers of his desk were stacked atop the desk where his computer had normally sat. All his papers seemed to have vanished.

But had they found all of Darrell's hidey-holes? She didn't expect that they would have.

The closet in his office was long and narrow with shelves along either side. Mostly, the shelves held boxes of old books and tax records, some supplies as well as his sports equipment. The thing she was interested in was still in place, though. An open cardboard box with two baseball gloves, a couple of balls and a baseball cap was in the rear corner just where it should have been. She knelt and pulled the box out from the wall and then pressed her fingers into the corner and felt the floorboards. She counted three boards from the corner. The third one came up if you knew where to push on it.

Beneath the board was a space large enough for a file folder to stand upright. There were two such folders hidden inside, and Tess withdrew both of them, stepped back quickly and sat in the desk chair with them.

The first folder held handwritten notes, mostly concerning land deals with Downey Construction. There was no financial information in the folder, just dates, names of people and lists of various lots of land.

The second folder held the printouts to accompany the notes. This was the first time she'd ever heard of Cage and Ventura except from Tommy Mott, and her first cursory glance answered many of her questions.

Cage and Ventura was, as she had assumed, a holding company, but it was really just a front for Downey Construction. The purchase money came from Downey through Jay Sturgis, the very man who had approached Tess in the parking lot that afternoon. The title to the property Darrell had bought was held by Cage and Ventura, but the truth was that Downey Construction held title to the land all along.

Darrell had been buying property for over three years, much of it going into her name at the time of purchase. So it was clear now that he hadn't remembered to get all of it signed over to him when they'd divorced. Could he actually have forgotten?

No, he hadn't forgotten. Not Darrell. He had purposefully left it in her name. She had no idea why he had done such a thing, but he wasn't the type to make a mistake like this. No, he'd left things just as he had wanted them. Unfortunately, he'd been killed before he was able to complete whatever scheme he'd been working on.

She needed more time to examine the documents, and she couldn't do it here, so she rolled the folders into a tube and stuffed them into her straw tote and prepared to leave.

Back in the living room, she noticed a second car parked outside. A dark sedan with tinted windows sat behind her old car, but there was no sign of the driver. It definitely wasn't a police car. That much was certain.

She froze, staring at the mysterious vehicle and listening for any sound of someone inside the house. *Nothing.*

Tess began backing away from the front door slowly, then with increasing speed, until she turned and ran back to the office and threw open the door to the beach. That was her undoing.

"Hey, lady! What's your hurry?"

A man rushed at her from the side, captured her in a bear hug and lifted her off the ground. She thrashed in his grip, but it was no use. He'd locked his arms around her and wasn't about to let go.

"What do you want?" she cried out. "Put me down!"

"We're just going to do a little business," the man insisted. He carried her back through the house to the front door. "You've got some papers to sign, and then you'll be on your way."

"I don't know about any land! It was Darrell's scam!"

"So you have to tie it up for him, that's all." They stepped through the front door, then stopped. A second man lay on the ground beside the driver's door of the sedan. Blood flowed from his scalp behind his left ear. "What's this?" The man released her, dropping her to the ground. "What's going on?"

He received his reply in the form of a solid blow to the back of the head. The man fell to his face on the ground.

Tess spun around, ready to run. She saw Charles Dumont, standing there with a baseball bat in his hand and grinning at her like the Cheshire cat.

"Home run," he said.

Chapter Seventeen

A shout of alarm can carry a great distance. But even beyond the range of hearing, fear can be felt. The sudden anxiety, the hair rising on the back of the neck for no reason . . . fear is a tangible thing, electric and alive, that crosses all boundaries physical and psychic.

Tess's fear rippled through the waters of the gulf like the shock of an ocean earthquake, and her alarm was notice to all who could feel the passing wave.

For Gabriel, the sudden and unmistakable feeling of Tess's fear was a beacon toward which his spirit could fly to find his love. The water became a blur that burst into sunshine as he flowed along the fading signal she'd sent out. In a few brief moments, he was moving to the white stucco house and behind the running figures of Tess and Charles Dumont.

He was there when they leaped into the banker's car and sped away; he was with them in their flight north along Sandhook Road to the house where he'd been that afternoon. He clung to her like a mist as she sat with her bag clutched to her chest and tried to collect her thoughts. *I'm here! Listen to me, lass. I'm*

*not dead! I am with you as always if you'll just bring
me back. Call for me! Believe in me!*

But Tess's mind was filled with other things, horrible thoughts and impressions that spilled over to
Gabriel's mind. The dead lawyer and Darrell's ill-
conceived land manipulations and the attack at the
house all jostled together in Tess's mind as she stared
numbly at the ocean and wondered what she could do
now.

There was no room for grief or remembrance in her
thoughts at the moment.

"YOU'LL BE SAFE HERE," Charles said to her as he
handed her a cup of tea and sat beside her on the
couch. "Now, what was going on?"

Tess looked around the paneled room at the sailing pictures on the walls and the books that filled the
bookcases and wondered if she should tell him or not.
What, for that matter, did she really know to tell? If
she didn't tell Charles, whom could she trust? Her
new partner, Tommy Mott? No, they'd surely be
watching him—they owned his mortgage after all—
and he couldn't help her anyway. Charles was the only
one she had now... now that Gabriel was gone.

The thought of the dashing pirate was like a rush of
sea air through her brain, a wave of yearning saying
Call for me! Believe in me! Oh, God, if only it were
that easy. Still, the thought of him calmed her and she
decided to tell the banker what she knew.

"My husband was apparently doing his best to
cheat a crooked businessman," she told Charles. "I
don't know what he was up to, but he was playing fast

and loose on a land deal and they killed him for it. Now they're after me, too.''

So she told him the tale as best she knew it, leaving nothing out except the part about the treasure at the bottom of the sea. Just as she began to tell him about that, she felt a sudden constriction, as though someone had clamped a hand over her mouth. And then the amulet in the pocket of her slacks seemed to grow warm. It was as if an unseen presence were guarding Gabriel's treasure, waiting to pounce on anyone wanting a share of the spoils.

When she'd finished her story, she sat back feeling exhausted. Charles Dumont studied the papers she'd taken from Darrell's home office.

''Sell it to me,'' he said after a moment.

''What?''

''Sell the property to me and I'll visit this Downey fellow for you. He'll buy it from whoever has possession and then he'll leave you alone.''

''Why would he leave me alone?''

''Can you prove those men were sent by him? Can you even identify them? No.'' He shook his head, smiling. ''He's desperate, otherwise he'd never have resorted to strong-arm tactics. But once he's gotten what he wants, he'll forget you.''

''I doubt that.''

''Please, Tess. This isn't a vendetta. It's only business. You can't prove a thing about him.''

''But I can, too. I've got the paperwork to prove a lot about him.''

''He doesn't know that. You get rid of that land and then leave these papers where the police will find them. That way he'll never know it was you that exposed his scheme.''

"I've got to take this to the police right now," Tess said. "There's no sense fooling around."

"No, but face it, Tess. You've still got legal hurdles to get over. These few sheets of paper won't change that."

Tess could see that he was right. The events of the day and the prospect of more trouble to come suddenly seemed like too much to cope with. She was so tired that she just couldn't think anymore. All she wanted to do was go to sleep and hope it would all go away.

"How did those guys know where to find you?" Charles asked.

"I suppose they followed me."

"And where were the police? I thought they were following you."

"I don't know," she admitted. "I just don't know."

Charles smiled and patted her shoulder consolingly. "You hungry?"

"Yes, I guess I am."

"I'll fix something for us," he offered. "You rest a bit and I'll be right back."

Tess watched the ocean rolling onto the beach in front of the house. The sky was blue, the threatening clouds having dissipated. It was as if nature was mocking her troubles, proving that the world kept turning without Gabriel just as it would continue no matter what happened to her.

The room she was in didn't really match the man. It was dark despite the large picture windows, and the paneled walls gave it a gloomy feeling that was contrary to Charles's breezy demeanor. It was obvious that he hadn't given much thought to redecorating since moving into the house.

Well, he just had better things to do, that's all. Why else would you buy a house with all its furnishings except to avoid having to decorate?

She hadn't seen much beyond the entrance and this room, for he'd herded her in rather quickly after their escape from Downey's ruffians. She knew there was a deck on the second floor because it formed the roof of the patio outside the front window. The deck was probably accessed through the master bedroom. This was the only house along the beach with a second-floor deck on the ocean. There seemed to be something important about that...

Tess let her eyes shut as she listened to the sound of the surf. The rhythm of the waves was soothing, and she let it lull her as she lay back against the corner of the overstuffed couch. It would be so nice to sleep.

Trying to sort things out in her tired mind was pointless. Besides, it was clear now that Carl Downey had had Darrell killed. All that remained was to prove it. She fell asleep wondering how the evidence she had might convince the police to turn their attention to Carl Downey.

"WHERE DID YOU TWO LEARN surveillance? Or, did you learn?" Detective Sergeant Wilkes turned from one to the other of the plainclothes officers as if trying to decide which one to strike first. "Maybe we should give you a three-wheeler and a chalk marker and put you on traffic patrol. How in hell did you lose a woman alone in a boat on the gulf? How?"

"Sir, we—"

"Never mind. Get out of here and find her! Find her or I'll have you guarding school crossings for the next ten years!"

He turned and stormed away from the two men, slamming the door to the squad room on his way out. Just when he was ready to haul her in with evidence that would stick, his men lost her. It wasn't fair.

He picked up the manila folder on his desk and smiled, saying softly to himself, "Okay, Teresa Miller, I've got your motive here, honey. I've got you right where your lawyer can't help you."

The best way to find a suspect was through the suspect's lawyer. No lawyer, especially an ambulance chaser like Chambers, wanted to be caught aiding a fugitive from justice. Not when their own license was on the line. With that thought in mind, Sergeant Wilkes left the building.

CHARLES DUMONT STOOD in the middle of the living room watching Tess sleep, half-reclining in the corner of the couch. He smiled, then licked his lips quickly. The drug he'd put in her tea was mild, but it would keep her knocked out for a couple of hours while he took care of business.

It would be so easy to get rid of her right now. So easy.

But if he did, he'd never know why she was in that boat this afternoon. Curiosity more than anything else had gotten him as far as this. And his curiosity had never failed to produce a profit.

Charles Dumont had been christened William Henry Clay thirty-six years earlier, but that name had become too well known to law enforcement officials in the New England states, so he was forced to choose another. Dumont was a good name for a man in his line of work because there was, indeed, a banking family named Dumont in Boston.

Charles Dumont's actual line of work had changed over the years, too. He'd started with petty theft and graduated to grand theft auto and breaking and entering. Then a brief stay in the Maine State Correctional Facility had brought him into contact with criminals of a slightly better class. "With your looks, you should be working the con," they'd told him. "It's a lot less work than jimmying locks after midnight and you can afford better lawyers if you get caught."

He had never been one for taking advice from his elders, but he took that advice and had done well with it. Charles Dumont had done very well indeed.

He was smart, too. Smart enough and curious enough to learn all he needed to know about business, the stock market and banking. Although he was a high school dropout, he could portray himself in any business role that suited his purpose. He always used a soft sell on his marks and pulled back if they showed reluctance. He never forced his hand and risked exposure.

Now, the name William Henry Clay was long forgotten. And as far as the police were concerned, he was just what he said he was, a respected Boston banker.

Looking down at Tess, he realized he had over-played his hand terribly this time, though. The intended victim hadn't been nearly as stupid or greedy as he expected him to be. And Charles should never have murdered Paul Driscoll on his balcony early Sunday morning. They'd argued and Charles had struck him without thought. If he had been thinking, he surely wouldn't have killed him in the light of the balcony doors. No, he'd been stupid.

And other mistakes had grown from that one mistake, leading him to compound the single murder into three. If he hadn't armed himself with that steak knife, he'd be on a flight out of the country right now. Instead, he'd killed twice more and there was still one more murder to commit.

But murder wasn't smart, and Charles had taken great care to act with extra intelligence since he'd killed Paul Driscoll. Even the unfortunate matter of running into Tess's ex-husband in the yard that night had been turned to his advantage by his quick thinking. And once Tess was found dead of suicide, her lawyer's death would make a certain amount of sense, as well.

And none of it would be tied to him. When Paul Driscoll's body was eventually found, there would be no link between it and Charles's earlier crimes. But he had to kill Tess tonight for his plan to work. Walter Chambers's body would be discovered in the morning.

Yes, he would kill Tess tonight, making sure to do a properly amateurish job of slitting her wrists. And if the cops didn't believe she'd committed suicide, the papers he would leave in her house would lead to Carl

Downey. In the morning, Charles would empty out his second bank account, fly directly to Jamaica and from there into obscurity. If he did return to this country, he would be using another name.

Charles Dumont was a murderer after all.

But he had to find out about the man in the boat first. And to do that, he had to maintain Tess's trust a bit longer.

Smiling benignly, Charles Dumont shifted Tess gently to lie on the couch and then covered her with a blanket. "Poor baby," he cooed, "you rest a bit while Charlie boy arranges to make some more money."

CARL DOWNEY WAS PACING the floor of his office, nervously chewing on a cigar. He'd tipped his hand with the strong-arm tactics, and now she'd hold him up for at least triple the price on the property. If she got the chance, that was. After all, people have accidents every day, don't they? All he needed from her was her signature.

The fact that she hadn't called the police in on the matter gave him faith that she was holding out for more money. If that was her intention, he could deal with her without much problem. All he had to do was find her.

TESS FELL DEEPLY into a trance, her mind taking her to the place where time and memory slipped into each other, and she was able to dream her way to the other side and glimpse fragments of long-ago events.

She dreamed a history; she dreamed a prophecy. And she dreamed of the death of Gabriel Dyer.

A wizened and frail African man lay on the woven mat in front of her, his ribs rising and falling erratically with his labored breathing. He looked up at her, motioning with one hand for her to kneel at his side. She did so, and he said something which she didn't understand.

"He's Kigani," someone said beside her, and she looked up at a bearded man. He wore loose cotton pants and a shirt, and a sword hung at his side on a sash. "A Congo tribe. Cannibals, I hear."

The African said something else, and she returned her gaze to him as he lifted his other hand, clutching something tightly in it.

"He wants you to have it," her companion said. "Magic, he calls it."

The African held his hand out again, opening it so that she could see the face of the amulet, the blood-red stone gleaming in the dim light of the hut.

She reached out to accept the gift, marveling as she did that her hand was broad and muscular, a man's hand. She noticed that the nails were dirty as the fingers closed around the carved face.

As he released the amulet, the Kigani tribesman smiled and relaxed. He closed his eyes and slept.

"He said it will protect you," the other man said. "Keep you alive. But these other fellows say he only gave it to you because none of them want any part of it."

Something in the man's smile put her on guard. He seemed amused by something.

She stood and held the amulet by the leather thong running through the eyelet atop the face. "Well, then," she said in Gabriel's fine baritone, "I'll take it gladly and wear it to guard me against the likes of you, Purcell.''

She felt herself lift the thong, hanging the amulet around her neck. It dropped against her skin...or was it Gabriel's muscular chest? The amulet felt cool and heavy against the skin at first, but then it grew warm.

For a moment, she felt incredibly alive. She felt the blood coursing through Gabriel's body, felt the strength in his arms and legs. And then the feeling faded and she felt as though she was slipping out of the body and up through the grass roof of the hut to the sky above the forest.

And a dark-skinned woman was speaking to her, her words muffled by time as though they were too private to be shared with a stranger. She held out a ribbon of fine red silk and smiled. Tess felt like crying when she saw the love in this woman's eyes and felt the touch of her hand on Gabriel's cheek and her kiss on his lips.

But there was no time for tears because she was suddenly assailed by wind on the tossing deck of the Maria Louisa. The man called Purcell was standing at the head of a gang of sailors, brandishing a cutlass. ''That black fellow called it the Ghost Maker,'' Purcell was saying. ''Said you had to give it away before you died or you'll linger on earth as a spirit. No one here will take it, you bloody fool, just as we will no longer abide your company. Goodbye, Captain Dyer!''

Suddenly, she was falling through the air, wind and rain tearing at her clothing and the amulet spilling out of her shirt as she hit the rolling sea and slipped beneath the waves.

She sank quickly, carried down by the weight of leather boots and waterlogged clothing, while her lungs burned with the pressure of the stale air inside them. "Sweet Mary, Mother of God, preserve this sinner on the waves. Mary, Mother of God, save me," Gabriel thought. Over and over, he thrashed frantically but without coordination until he hit the bottom of the gulf.

It was Tess who grasped the amulet in both hands, thinking, "God rest my soul." She released the burning air and let the water in. She was so tired, and it seemed so warm beneath the waves.

And then all was darkness as she began to float back into her own world once more.

Save me. Believe in me. A voice in the darkness, a whispering in her ear. *Call me and believe.* The voice of her desires—Gabriel's voice—warmed the void around her. *I'm here, lass. I've not gone yet. Call me.* She dreamed that a flutter of silken ribbon fell into her hand, and she grasped it as a talisman of the man who wore it. Such a lovely dream. She could almost believe he was still with her, but she knew it was all just a dream. *Necklace.* What? *Necklace.* It made no sense at all.

But it was only a dream after all.

SERGEANT WILKES OPENED the door to Walter Chambers's office. He found the lawyer still seated inside just as Charles Dumont was approaching the parking lot in front of the Downey Construction offices. All while Tess slept on.

Chapter Eighteen

Tess lay wrapped in the ancient rhythms, surrounded by the gentle ebb and flow of the ocean tides, the hoofbeats of animals roaming the African veld and the insect chirr of the jungle. She felt herself lifted by it all, buoyed out of confusion into certainty as she rose from the depth of her sleep. She awoke to the rays of sunset over the gulf thinking, "The view from upstairs must be wonderful at this time of day."

She was lying on the couch, a light blanket covering her. She felt lethargic and didn't want to move even to turn her eyes away from the sun.

It was very considerate of Charles to cover her like this and not wake her. Of course, he'd been her knight in shining armor today, hadn't he, coming to her rescue like that? Really, much more considerate than she'd expected.

Tess lifted her hand to cover her eyes, and as she did, something fell against the back of her hand, brushing it as lightly as a spider walking across her skin. She moved her hand back again, examining it. A length of ribbon hung through her fingers, the red silk faded to a dusty pink.

For a moment, she didn't recognize what it was, then it was suddenly all too clear. *Gabriel's ribbon!*

As she stared at it, the dream came flooding back to her. She had been in Gabriel's body, experiencing episodes of his life just as he had once experienced them. She remembered it now, all of it, but she didn't know how or why she'd had such a dream.

She remembered the old man who gave him the amulet, recalling especially the look of desperation in his eyes when he held it out to Gabriel. He had been pleading in his language for Gabriel to take the amulet. Pleading for someone to take the accursed token away from him lest he should die with it in his possession. For whatever protection the amulet may have given him in life, he knew that in death it would be a curse to him.

Tess suspected that the man whom Gabriel had called Purcell had left something out of his translation. There had clearly been a grudge between them, and the man had withheld the reason the local tribe didn't want to accept the amulet.

She knew this story as though it was a memory of her own, but she had no idea why the ribbon was in her hand or how it came to be there. What did it mean?

She clutched the ribbon tightly and sat up on the couch. It meant something, and she could only hope it meant something good. But for the moment, it seemed to mean that she had to get moving.

"Charles?" she called out. "Are you here?"

There was no response, no sound at all.

"Charles?" Still nothing. She was obviously alone in the house. And then she remembered what she had been thinking when she awoke. Something about the view from the upper balcony.

She had been thinking that it had to have been this balcony that she'd seen from the water. Charles's balcony. And if that was the case...

She headed upstairs. It was clear Charles had done no decorating since moving in. The place was all darkly paneled, with a nautical theme. Tess found the bedroom easily enough, then stepped out onto the upper deck as the sun was half-submerged in the gulf.

Yes, if someone had been on this deck, with the light of the bedroom on, she could have seen them from the water. Looking in both directions, she could see no other second-floor decks or balconies. It had to have been this house! A ground-level patio wouldn't have been visible from her vantage point in the water.

It must have been this house. This very house! And there had been two men, not just Charles, but two men.

Who was the other man?

Tess turned toward the bedroom again. Was the second man Paul Driscoll, the previous owner? She would have to find out where he lived now and ask.

As she stepped toward the sliding glass door, a reflection low on the floor beside the wall caught her eye—a single semaphore flash. Tess stooped and groped around in what was fast becoming full night. She found a piece of glass, a bit smaller than palm-size, nearly flat and smooth. Taking it into the bedroom, she switched on the light and examined her find.

It was the lens from a pair of eyeglasses. Bifocals.

Tess slipped the lens into the pocket of her slacks. It clinked against the amulet, reminding her of the ribbon she still carried wrapped around her right hand.

In the bedroom, she opened the closet. It was full of suits, mostly gray or dark blue, and there were several pairs of dress shoes. Nothing casual in there, just business. That didn't seem like Charles.

Just as she was about to close the closet door, a glimmer of light amid the shoes caused her to kneel and pull out a framed photograph. It was an eight-by-ten photograph of an older man with two young girls at his side shot from the waist up. He was gray-haired, smiling and wearing a dark suit like the ones above her. He wore glasses. And peering closely at the photograph, she could see—yes, he was wearing bifocals.

Tess dropped the photograph as though it had stung her. She stood and slammed the closet door. Bifocals and a dark suit. A man who looked like the type to want a darkly paneled house and nautical prints on his walls. It must have been a picture of Paul Driscoll.

She could imagine a man selling his house with all his furnishings, but she could not imagine him leaving without trying to find the missing lens of his glasses...

So why had he?

And why had Charles said he hadn't been on the deck with his light on when it was so obvious that his was the only light she could have seen so clearly?

Something I saw, she thought, *or something that somebody thinks I saw.* And if somebody thought she saw something, might it not be prudent for him to become friendly with her to find out if she did, indeed, see anything? Maybe he'd want to keep a close eye on her—even to the point of sneaking around her house in the dead of night.

Tess froze, holding the ribbon like a rosary to drive her sudden fear away.

CHARLES DUMONT WAS SEATED quite comfortably in the leather chair across the desk from Carl Downey.

"You offered her one hundred thousand dollars," he was saying, "but I'll get you the property for half that."

"Why?" Carl smiled, knowing a con man when he saw one. "Why will you do me this great favor for less than I'm willing to pay?"

"I'm not greedy."

"The hell you aren't." Carl laughed. "What's the angle?"

"The angle is that I have to leave town in the morning and I want to be sure of two things. One, that I am paid tonight. Two, that I keep you happy enough so that you don't interfere with my departure."

"What you mean is that you've made a bundle off some other scam, so this is only a little bonus on your way out of the country."

"Whatever." Charles shrugged. "Do we have a deal?"

"We do. You bring the paper back signed and I'll have your money here for you."

"Very good." Charles stood and took the deed from the desk. "Don't follow me, Carl. Your boys scared the hell out of her this afternoon, and I'd hate them to screw it up now."

"I won't follow you," Carl said. "But if you don't make good, I'll sure as hell find you."

"Well, then, we understand each other. Goodbye."

As soon as Charles left the room, Carl Downey was on the phone. "He's on his way down. Give him plenty of room, but don't lose him. I have to get the paper back as soon as she signs it." There was no way Carl Downey was going to let some fake banker hold his project for ransom after the deed was signed.

THINK! NO, SHE JUST couldn't remember exactly what she'd seen from the water on Saturday night. Just two men on the upper deck. Two men, and then the light went out.

Tess was hurrying through the house looking for something, anything, that might tell her what he was trying to cover up. But there was nothing to jog her memory or give her a clue, and everywhere she looked, there was further evidence that Charles Dumont had never lived in this house.

"Oh, Gabriel, I sure need you now," she whispered, hastening down to the main floor and through the living room. "Please come back."

Though she didn't believe he could, she felt for a moment his presence beside her. No, more correctly, in her mind. *Necklace,* she thought he said, just as he'd said in her dream. Necklace? It made no sense at all.

In the kitchen Tess glanced over the countertops, scanning appliances and racks of knives. She opened and shut drawers without knowing what she was searching for. She made a circuit of the room wondering if she should wait for Charles to return or run while she could, wondering why the word "necklace" had popped into her head, wondering why she was still looking when she didn't know what she wanted to find.

And then she found it.

The kitchen had a restaurant-size freezer that opened from the top. She pulled the door open. Just as quickly, she shut it. Paul Driscoll's body was inside.

"Oh, God!" she cried out. "Oh, oh, no!" She rushed to the wall phone and dialed 911. "Hello, yes, I want to report a murder. Yes, a—" But the front door opened, and she heard footsteps approaching. She let the phone drop and backed away as quietly as possible.

Unfortunately, there was only the wall behind her, and all hope of escape lay across the room. Tess didn't stop to think but bolted toward the kitchen door, hoping against hope to avoid Charles, to reach the door and the safety of a public street.

But Charles caught up to her before she could run out, and he pulled her back into the kitchen. She found herself looking at the barrel of a gun aimed directly at her head!

"Hang it up," Charles said, motioning with the gun for her to hang up the phone. "Good. Now sit."

Tess sat at the table.

"Right. You will do two things for me, Tess. One, you will sign this paper," he said, laying the deed on the table before her. "And you will explain your actions in the boat today."

"And what do I get?" There was no way on earth that she intended to sign the paper. It would surely be the same as signing her own death warrant.

"You get out with your life."

"I don't believe you."

"You think I'll kill you?"

"You've killed everyone else," she said. She felt calmer now, the certainty that he intended to kill her no matter what she did giving her strength. "I assume that Darrell was an accident, but I doubt that Paul Driscoll was. And I know that Walter Chambers wasn't."

"Well, they all were, in a way." He put one foot up on the chair across the table from her and leaned on his knee. "Poor Paul Driscoll tried to back out of our deal. I got carried away. That wouldn't have mattered if I hadn't run into you on the beach. And once I knew you'd spent the night there, well, I had to make sure I wasn't leaving any loose ends."

"I'm the only loose end left," she said. "It's too bad your little suicide plan didn't work out for you."

Necklace, a voice seemed to be saying in the back of her mind. *Necklace.* Why?

"Yes, too bad. You put up quite a fight. How did you manage that?"

"That would be three things you want from me. You said only two."

Necklace! Believe!

"Right. About the boat, then. I'm quite curious."

"I was diving for treasure."

"Oh, of course." He laughed.

"Here, I'll show you." Tess slouched down a bit in her chair so she could slip her hand into the pocket of her slacks to retrieve the coins. She grasped the coins and amulet, pulling them free, and a sudden sensation of vertigo struck her.

Wrong, lass! A necklace is needed! Believe! The words hammered through her head as she held the amulet in her hand, and she nearly dropped everything. She recovered and sat up again. Yes, that was the answer. A necklace! That's why she had the ribbon! She gently dropped the amulet on the chair between her legs and placed two coins on the table before her captor.

Charles focused on the coins and paid no attention to Tess. Under the table, she unwound the ribbon and began trying to slip it through the eyelet in the stone.

"It's too bad I've got to be going," Charles said, holding one of the coins up to the light. "If there's much of this, it would be worth millions."

"There's a lot more," Tess assured him, as she continued trying to thread the stone. "A whole ship."

"Not for me, I'm afraid," he said ruefully. "But I guess I did well enough. What about the man in the boat? What happened to him?"

"Man?" She almost had it now, struggling to grasp the ribbon with her fingertips without looking at it.

"Don't pull that on me." He dropped the coin and raised the gun once more. "The man who disappeared. He dropped a stone of some kind, I think."

"Oh, that man." Tess smiled, finally pulling the ribbon through. "He's gone." She tied the ribbon with a square knot, hoping the resultant necklace was large enough without her being able to look at it. Then, in sudden inspiration, she raised her hands and laid the stone on the table before her. "I do have his amulet, however."

"Shove it over here." Greed lit Charles's eyes as he looked at the carved image threaded with the faded ribbon.

"Gabriel," Tess said. "Come back, Gabriel."

"What?"

That was all Charles said, however, for the red stone in the amulet suddenly gleamed and the necklace shook and then twisted on the table. Both he and Tess stared for a moment in silence while the world seemed to stop on its axis. Then the amulet slid across tabletop with a harsh, grinding sound, flew into the air and hung there from the ribbon for just a moment.

Then it was as though the motes of dust in the air congealed and darkened into a human form. A man took shape, clothed in a silk shirt and dark trousers, with heavy leather boots up to his knees and at his side a sword hanging from a red sash.

Gabriel shook back his mane of hair and laughed. "Yes!" But he didn't pause to enjoy his transformation, or even to look at Tess, but swiftly drew out his weapon. "Run, lass! I'll handle this fool!"

Charles jumped back in confusion and fright, instinctively raising his gun and firing blindly as he staggered away. The bullet was wide of the target, but Gabriel's sword wasn't. It cut a stripe across the con man's jacket as he turned to flee.

Gabriel gave chase, cutting off Charles's path to the front door. Charles spun wildly, firing once more, then ran toward the door to the beach. Gabriel's sword pricked his back, urging him out to the sand, where he rolled down the hill to the moonlit surf.

"You're mine, Dumont," Gabriel shouted. "You'll not get away."

Tess ran after the two men, afraid of the gun Charles still clutched. Afraid, too, that Gabriel might kill him. When she reached the door, however, there were two other men running toward the combatants.

The newcomers joined the melee, one of them falling at a swipe of Gabriel's sword, the other shooting at Charles. "No, wait!" Charles was shouting as Tess reached the top of the hill. "I'm not going anywhere!"

"You're right," one of the men called back.

"He cut me! That other guy cut me!" the second one cried out.

Gabriel turned away from Charles and Charles raised his weapon as Tess screamed, "Gabriel! Look out!"

There were three shots, and Tess started running, heedless of any danger to herself. Gabriel dived and rolled and came up staggering, then lunged at Charles with his sword. But Charles was already falling, struck by a shot from one of the men who were now running up toward their car. Gabriel fell to his face in the sand.

"No!" Tess cried, kneeling at Gabriel's side. "Not again!" She turned him over, amazed at the blood on his chest, dark in the moonlight. "Don't die! Don't leave me!"

"I shan't be leaving you," Gabriel said, his breath coming in ragged gasps. Then he pushed himself up with a groan, staggered a couple of steps and fell to his knees near Charles Dumont.

"What are you doing?" Tess asked. "Lie still now."

"Dumont, you bloody fool, you don't want to die, do you?"

"No," Charles gasped. Blood dribbled from his lips. "Get help."

"I've got your help here," Gabriel said. "It's kept me alive and it'll do the same for you. Will you take it, man?"

"What?" The question was feeble, barely a whisper.

"Will you take this amulet to keep from dying? Will you accept it as my gift?"

"Yes," Charles moaned. "Anything. Please, yes."

"Then I give it to you," Gabriel said, lifting the necklace from his own neck. "I give you this precious ornament to keep you here, Charles Dumont. It's certainly what you deserve." He slipped it around Charles's neck just before the man's eyes slid shut.

Tess knelt beside him, staring at the banker. "Gabriel, what have you done?"

"I've saved my hide and damned his soul," the pirate replied. Then he turned toward her and said, "See?" He stretched out his arms.

The blood was gone from his chest, the bullet wound healed.

"Oh, Gabriel!" Tess threw herself into his solid, warm embrace. "But he's dead. It didn't save him."

"Oh, but I'm sure that it did. Just as it saved me," he told her. "He's around somewhere."

The growing wail of a siren broke them apart then, and Tess stood, looking up toward the house. "You'd better get out of here," she told him. "I don't know how to explain you to the police."

"Yes, 'twould be awkward." Gabriel took the necklace from Charles's neck and stood with it. "I'll take this away with me."

"Don't touch it!"

"Never you worry, lass. I don't own the thing any longer," he assured her. "I gave it away and it no longer has any power over me."

"Then you're alive? Really alive?"

"Yes, I am at that. And I'll never leave you, dar-lin' Tess, never through all eternity."

Epilogue

The sun set over the Gulf of Mexico with a magnificent burst of yellow-orange light that darkened to deep red at the horizon. Tess stood on the deck of the *Maria Louisa II* and watched the sun sinking into the sea, feeling as though she was alive for the first time in her life. Alive and content.

There was a time when she didn't think she would ever be feeling anywhere near this good. No, Sergeant Wilkes had tried his best to lock her up for good despite the mounting evidence against Charles Dumont. Eventually, however, even he had to admit she was blameless in her husband's death. Tess figured he'd finally given up on her when they discovered that Darrell's estate was only a paper one. All that Tess stood to inherit were his debts.

Claiming salvage rights to the *Maria Louisa* was far easier than she had expected. All they had to do was bring up something from the ship proving its identity and they could claim the wreck as theirs. There were massive taxes to be paid, of course, but nothing compared to the finds. Workmen and marine historians were salvaging the ship's cargo now, while she and Gabriel took their honeymoon cruise on the two-masted sailboat they'd bought with the first of their proceeds.

And so here they were, just the two of them, on the wide expanse of the ocean.

"A lovely view, isn't it?" Gabriel came to her side, his arm slipping around her as he tipped his head to rest it on her shoulder. "The lure of the sea."

"I understand why sailors love it," Tess said. "The whole world is open to you just over the horizon."

"And what's behind you is over the horizon, as well," he replied. "Which was always as much motivation to sail as the lure of what lies ahead."

"And what does lie ahead?" She snuggled against him, rubbing her cheek against the crown of his head.

"Great things, my dear. We're destined for great things," he proclaimed. "When the remainder of the ship's treasure has been brought up, we'll have the world at our feet."

"I don't need the world at my feet," she told him. "Not right at the moment anyway."

He turned her to him, kissing her cheeks. "You have me at your feet."

"And I am at yours."

"Then everything is perfect." He held her to him as they watched the sun set together. "Or, nearly perfect."

"Why only nearly?"

"We have one piece of unfinished business, lass," he said. "One task only."

Gabriel withdrew a small bundle from his pocket and unwrapped the paper around it. The amulet lay within, the red stone glowing dully.

"I thought perhaps now might be the time to be rid of it."

"Oh, Gabriel, does he deserve to be lost so far at sea? I mean, Charles was a con man and a murderer, but it seems so cruel."

"Aye, lass, that it is," he agreed. "But as I was freed from the spell, so might he be one day, and whoever lets him out could well be the next one captured by it. Better to abandon a scoundrel now than to risk a better person being trapped next time."

"I suppose you're right."

"Oh, yes, I am right. Besides, he might learn a bit of humanity after a few hundred years of watching the fish swim by. Shall I drop the accursed thing and be done with it, Mrs. Dyer?"

"Yes, Mr. Dyer, for I don't want him watching over us tonight," she said with a grin. "I don't want anyone watching at all."

"Aye, privacy we'll have, milady. And tomorrow, I'll teach you how to sail this marvelous sailboat of ours."

"And we'll sail around the world together forever."

"Yes, my love, forever."

He let the amulet slip from his hand to the waves and then took the centuries-old ribbon and placed it in her hand. "For you, love, to bind your beautiful hair."

"She wouldn't mind?"

"She would surely approve. I love you, Tess, and love grants its approval."

The sun disappeared beneath the horizon as they embraced. Above them, the stars came out like the thousand eyes of ancient benevolent gods, keeping watch over the lovers in the night.

Weddings by DeWilde

Since the turn of the century the elegant and fashionable DeWilde stores have helped brides around the world turn the fantasy of their "Special Day" into reality. But now the store and three generations of family are torn apart by the divorce of Grace and Jeffrey DeWilde. As family members face new challenges and loves—and a long-secret mystery—the lives of Grace and Jeffrey intermingle with store employees, friends and relatives in this fast-paced, glamorous, internationally set series. For weddings and romance, glamour and fun-filled entertainment, enter the world of DeWilde...

Twelve remarkable books, coming to you once a month, beginning in April 1996

Weddings by DeWilde begins with
Shattered Vows
by Jasmine Cresswell

Here's a preview!

"SPEND THE NIGHT with me, Lianne."

No softening lies, no beguiling promises, just the curt offer of a night of sex. She closed her eyes, shutting out temptation. She had never expected to feel this sort of relentless drive for sexual fulfillment, so she had no mechanisms in place for coping with it. "No." The one-word denial was all she could manage to articulate.

His grip on her arms tightened as if he might refuse to accept her answer. Shockingly, she wished for a split second that he would ignore her rejection and simply bundle her into the car and drive her straight to his flat, refusing to take no for an answer. All the pleasures of mindless sex, with none of the responsibility. For a couple of seconds he neither moved nor spoke. Then he released her, turning abruptly to open the door on the passenger side of his Jaguar. "I'll drive you home," he said, his voice hard and flat. "Get in."

The traffic was heavy, and the rain started again as an annoying drizzle that distorted depth perception made driving difficult, but Lianne didn't fool herself that the silence inside the car was caused by the driving conditions. The air around them crackled and sparked with their thwarted desire. Her body was still on fire. Why didn't Gabe say something? she thought, feeling aggrieved.

Perhaps because he was finding it as difficult as she was to think of something appropriate to say. He was thirty years old, long past the stage of needing to bed a woman just so he could record another sexual conquest in his little black book. He'd spent five months dating Julia, which suggested he was a man who valued friendship as an element in his relationships with women. Since he didn't seem to like her very much, he was probably as embarrassed as she was by the stupid, inexplicable intensity of their physical response to each other.

"Maybe we should just set aside a weekend to have wild, uninterrupted sex," she said, thinking aloud. "Maybe that way we'd get whatever it is we feel for each other out of our systems and be able to move on with the rest of our lives."

His mouth quirked into a rueful smile. "Isn't that supposed to be my line?"

"Why? Because you're the man? Are you sexist enough to believe that women don't have sexual urges? I'm just as aware of what's going on between us as you are, Gabe. Am I supposed to pretend I haven't noticed that we practically ignite whenever we touch? And that we have nothing much in common except mutual lust—and a good friend we betrayed?"

HARLEQUIN®

Don't miss these Harlequin favorites by some of our most distinguished authors!
And now, you can receive a discount by ordering two or more titles!

HT #25645	THREE GROOMS AND A WIFE by JoAnn Ross	$3.25 U.S./$3.75 CAN. ☐
HT #25648	JESSIE'S LAWMAN by Kristine Rolofson	$3.25 U.S./$3.75 CAN. ☐
HP #11725	THE WRONG KIND OF WIFE by Roberta Leigh	$3.25 U.S./$3.75 CAN. ☐
HP #11755	TIGER EYES by Robyn Donald	$3.25 U.S./$3.75 CAN. ☐
HR #03382	THE BABY BUSINESS by Rebecca Winters	$2.99 U.S./$3.50 CAN. ☐
HR #03375	THE BABY CAPER by Emma Goldrick	$2.99 U.S./$3.50 CAN. ☐
HS #70638	THE SECRET YEARS by Margot Dalton	$3.75 U.S./$4.25 CAN. ☐
HS #70655	PEACEKEEPER by Marisa Carroll	$3.75 U.S./$4.25 CAN. ☐
HI #22280	MIDNIGHT RIDER by Laura Pender	$2.99 U.S./$3.50 CAN. ☐
HI #22235	BEAUTY VS THE BEAST by M.J. Rogers	$3.50 U.S./$3.99 CAN. ☐
HAR #16531	TEDDY BEAR HEIR by Elda Minger	$3.50 U.S./$3.99 CAN. ☐
HAR #16596	COUNTERFEIT HUSBAND by Linda Randall Wisdom	$3.50 U.S./$3.99 CAN. ☐
HH #28795	PIECES OF SKY by Marianne Willman	$3.99 U.S./$4.50 CAN. ☐
HH #28855	SWEET SURRENDER by Julie Tetel	$4.50 U.S./$4.99 CAN. ☐

(limited quantities available on certain titles)

	AMOUNT	$
DEDUCT:	**10% DISCOUNT FOR 2+ BOOKS**	$
ADD:	**POSTAGE & HANDLING**	$
	($1.00 for one book, 50¢ for each additional)	
	APPLICABLE TAXES**	$_____
	TOTAL PAYABLE	$_____
	(check or money order—please do not send cash)	

To order, complete this form and send it, along with a check or money order for the total above, payable to Harlequin Books, to: **In the U.S.:** 3010 Walden Avenue, P.O. Box 9047, Buffalo, NY 14269-9047; **In Canada:** P.O. Box 613, Fort Erie, Ontario, L2A 5X3.

Name: _____

Address: _____ City: _____

State/Prov.: _____ Zip/Postal Code: _____

**New York residents remit applicable sales taxes.
  Canadian residents remit applicable GST and provincial taxes.

HBACK-AJ3

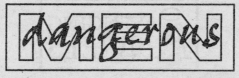

HARLEQUIN®

I N T R I G U E ®

Angels should have wings and flowing robes—not tight black jeans and leather jackets. They should be chubby cherubs or wizened old specters—not virile and muscular and sinfully sexy.

But then again, the AVENGING ANGELS aren't your average angels!

Enter the Denver Branch of Avenging Angels and meet some of the sexiest angels this side of heaven.

Sam—THE RENEGADE by Margaret St. George
(#358, February)

Dashiell—THE IMPOSTOR by Cassie Miles
(#363, March)

and the littlest angel-to-be
Ariel—THE CHARMER by Leona Karr
(#366, April)

Kiel—THE SOULMATE by Carly Bishop
(#370, May)

They may have a problem with earthly time—but these angels have no problem with earthly pleasures!

ANGEL1

Fall in love all over again with

This Time...
MARRIAGE

In this collection of original short stories, three brides get a unique chance for a return engagement!

- Being kidnapped from your bridal shower by a one-time love can really put a crimp in your wedding plans! *The Borrowed Bride*— by **Susan Wiggs**, *Romantic Times* Career Achievement Award-winning author.

- After fifteen years a couple reunites for the sake of their child—this time will it end in marriage? *The Forgotten Bride*—by **Janice Kaiser**.

- It's tough to make a good divorce stick—especially when you're thrown together with your ex in a magazine wedding shoot! *The Bygone Bride*— by **Muriel Jensen**.

Don't miss THIS TIME...MARRIAGE, available in April wherever Harlequin books are sold.

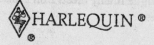

HARLEQUIN ®

Follow the trail of a baby boom...

MYSTERY BABY
by Dani Sinclair
in May

THE BABY EXCHANGE
by Kelsey Roberts
in June

A STRANGER'S BABY
by Susan Kearney
in July

It all begins when a MYSTERY BABY is thrust into a man's arms by a frantic woman, who then runs off. Next, THE BABY EXCHANGE occurs, where two babies and a secret lead to romance. And finally a new mother awakens to find herself faced with amnesia...and A STRANGER'S BABY.

For expectant readers only! LOST & FOUND...where babies and Intrigue finally meet! Don't miss any of them!

LNF